The Diamond Dunes Murders

A Phoenix Detective Mystery
Book #3

Shelly Young Bell

To Mom

With special thanks to Howard Gibb
of Howard Gibb Associates
and The Royal River Company
for the use of the Cape May postcard.

This is a work of fiction. It is not biographical nor autobiographical. All names, characters, places, and incidents are the product of the author's imagination or are used fictitiously, and any resemblance to actual persons living or dead, places or events is entirely coinciden

The Phoenix Detective Mysteries
A Very Sisterly Murder, Book 1
Murder at St. Katherine's, Book 2
The Diamond Dunes Murders, Book 3
The Cabot College Murders, Book 4
Population 10, The Dead End Murders, Book 5
R.S.V.P. to Murder, Book 6
Murder on the Promenade Deck, Book 7
Murder at 13 Curves, Book 8

Historic Novel
Stand Like the Brave

Copyright © 2019 Shelly Young Bell
Revised / Updated 2022
All Rights Reserved
ISBN-13: 9781650058351

What was supposed to be a lovely beach house party turns deadly. A group of friends old and new seeking sun and sand in Ocean City, New Jersey, find themselves hunting murderers, imposters and treasure and wondering who will be next. Secrets abound, but who will reveal what they know? Once again, Detective Ann Essex teams up with Detective Bill Dancer in this tale of deception, greed and death amongst the dunes.

Follow Detective Ann Essex, her associates Detectives Bill Dancer and Tom Van Pelt, best friends Suzanne and Che-Che, and investigative daughter Robin and her ever present friend Caela, as they solve murders and piece together the mysteries they encounter.

Prologue

"Mom"What?" Ann asked. Ann Essex had answered her cell phone when she saw it was her daughter, Robin, calling. Normally, she'd let a call during dinner go to voicemail. Robin was at Suzanne's Ocean City shore house with several other teen friends. They had planned to have pizza on the boardwalk and then ride whatever rides were working in the bad weather rather than join Ann and her adult friends in Cape May taking in the sights and having dinner.

"It's Suzanne, she's dead!"
Ann looked up and into Suzanne's eyes.
"What? Say that again," Ann asked Robin, trying to remain calm.
"It's Susanne, she's been murdered!" Robin cried.
"Robin, honey, Suzanne is sitting right here next to me."
"Mom, come! Please!"

Chapter 1

Four Days Earlier, July 2

Pack light, move fast. With that edict in mind, Bill Dancer contemplated his final clothing selections for the trip to Suzanne Beck's summer beach house, Diamond Dunes. Pack light, yes, but Bill wanted to be sure he was adequately covered for every possible social scenario. He studied the clothing taken from his lime scented drawers and laid out on his bed in the early morning light. The morning was golden and still, promising a clear, warm July day. Perfect beach weather. He needed to get all this packed in the next half hour. John and Ann Essex would soon be at the door of their gatehouse where he lived, ready to pick him up.

There would be a full laundry at the shore house, so Bill decided to pack only half of what he thought he needed for the week: four polo shirts, two seersucker button down short sleeve shirts, two khaki Bermuda shorts, one pair khaki slacks, two bathing suits, two beach shirts, docksider loafers and sandals so he could go sockless, a baseball cap, underwear, something to sleep in, and his bathroom kit. Bill hoped it was adequate. The email from Suzanne had pretty well laid out the informality of the week-long house party. The dressiest any of them need prepare for would be supper out at a local seafood or Italian place that would be filled with other casually dressed vacationers. Bill knew he had probably over packed and over thought the whole process, but a week with Suzanne?!!? He'd be under scrutiny the entire time, not only by Suzanne, but by Criminal Investigative Consultant Ann Essex, his coworker and previous boss. Bill dreaded the inevitable teasing over his wardrobe and sense of style, so he purposely had planned *not* to pack his handmade leather loafers, tailored shirts, or anything cashmere. Middle of the road clothing would be best. Bill was glad he had some clothes that would do, and he had recently purchased the rest, just for this occasion.

Satisfied with his final choices, Bill laid the carefully folded clothing into his small wheelie suitcase. He checked the time. He had better get a move on. Setting the suitcase by the door, he retrieved his cell phone charger and slid it into the outside zipper pocket of the suitcase. Bill returned to his bedroom of his upstairs carriage house apartment. He made sure all lights were off and the windows were locked there and in the adjoining bathroom. Once back in the combination living/kitchen area, he picked up a small cooler, set it on the pale tan granite countertop, and opened his apartment sized refrigerator. His pepper pineapple cheese balls were ready to pack along with the mixed veggies he'd chopped last night and stored in zipper bags. Suzanne had mentioned most evenings there'd be a nibble and a glass of wine before dinner. Bill had offered to bring the first evening's hors d'oeuvres.

Bill set the cooler by the suitcase, double checked that the refrigerator door was closed tightly, and that the coffee pot and toaster were unplugged. He flicked off the lights as he went down the staircase to his front door where he'd await John and Ann, teenage daughter Robin, and her constant companion, Caela.

An early morning start would not only get the five of them south on I-95 through Philadelphia before most of the rush hour traffic, but also would have them arrive at their good friend, Suzanne's, beach house by mid-morning. There would be plenty of time for a donut from Brown's on the boardwalk and a couple of hours on the beach before lunch.

John pulled up to the gatehouse at the end of their driveway, noting that Bill was ready and waiting. Good man, John thought to himself. Never keep your driver waiting. Ann had decided she'd sit in the back seat of the Jeep with Robin and Caela, leaving the shotgun seat for Bill so he could navigate. Not that he needed help, John thought to himself; they'd been to Suzanne's beach house before and it was easy to find. They would drive down I-95 to the Walt Whitman Bridge, south on Route 42 and the Atlantic City Expressway, south on the Garden State Parkway to the first of the two Ocean City exits. Then straight across the causeway which became 9th street. Suzanne's house was just above 2nd Street, on a quiet residential street, a mere block from the beach.

John had decided to stop at the Circle Liquor Store in Somers Point before crossing over from the mainland to the barrier island. Since Ocean City remained a 'dry' town, no liquor sales were allowed, thus making it possible to keep the resort town more 'family friendly' than many of the other more party-atmosphere communities. He'd pick up a few bottles of red and white wine, and a bottle of Suzanne's favorite vodka as a hostess gift. It would only take ten minutes. The girls lobbied that the stop was wasting valuable time. He'd be quick, and had planned their departure to arrive when the store opened at 9:00 a.m.. John slid his sunglasses on against the rising sun, and smoothed his graying hair at his temples. Once Bill was situated, John eased the Jeep out of the driveway and onto the road.

It turned out to be a quiet ride; each lost in their own thoughts and expectations for the week away together.

Ann had made and packed a large pan of lasagna for their dinner that first night to help out with the crowd that would be at Suzanne's all week. In addition to Suzanne, it would be Bill, John and herself, Robin and Caela, and their mutual friend, Florencia 'Che-Che' Rosita Maria Reyes. Tonight, they would eat in, and on the 4th of July they had all been invited next door to Suzanne's neighbor's barbeque. A couple of nights including one night in Cape May, they would eat out. Bill and John both had offered to pick up the dinner tabs for the nights they ate out. Che-Che would be making a Cuban themed supper one night. As good houseguests they had offered to help with the dinner preparations. Suzanne had been kind enough to ask them all 'down the shore' for the week, so they felt it was the least they could do. Ann looked forward to the diverse dinner offerings.

Ann rode along, squeezed in between Robin and Caela with her eyes shut against the sun which was full in their faces as they headed south and east. She had chosen not to wear a brimmed hat today in the car as she did not want to arrive at Suzanne's with her newly cropped, blonde hair all crumpled. Enough time for frizzy, windblown, uncombed hair during the week ahead. Ann loved the beach, and had very much looked forward to the trip since Suzanne had mentioned it last Christmas Day.

Christmas seemed like ages ago. Ann had recovered from her broken hip, spending as much time in physical therapy as the therapists thought she needed. They sent a set of exercises and big rubber bands home with her so she could continue the exercises to strengthen her hip and the muscles around it. It had been over six months and Ann was feeling mobile, if not 100% confident yet. No more chasing crooks down icy alleys!

Ann wasn't worried about this shortness of confidence. Her brain and spirit had returned to normal after that botched robbery case last December, and she felt her physical self-confidence would just require some additional time. She was getting around, but her hip became fatigued easily. Ann knew she just had to keep working at strengthening it. After all, she was the Phoenix – always rising above adversity. After she left the Philadelphia Police Department, she had hoped the moniker would be left behind. Alas, someone at the local Buckelsmere Police Department had learned of it so it was still occasionally brought up. Yes, she would try to always rise above anything that happened to her, even when the odds were against her.

She had left the Philadelphia Police Department and signed on as a 'Criminal Investigative Consultant' with the local Buckelsmere Police Department. This had given her a great deal more free time at home. Her quitting the Philadelphia Police Department luckily occurred right at the time that the Village of Buckelsmere was finalizing their next budget. Instead of trying to fit her salary as a full-time detective into the already tight Police allocation, the village of Buckelsmere was able to allocate some money for her occasional consultancy on extreme cases where they might need her expertise. This was proving a very good decision on her part. The three of them had settled into a new pattern at home these past few months, although that pattern had changed at the end of Robin's freshman year at the local high school. Robin would be home with her and John.

Robin would continue to take voice lessons over the summer, and had promised to read all the books on the suggested summer reading list for her sophomore English class. Yeah right! Ann thought to herself, let's see if that happens. There was good sense to having read all the texts before school started, then when it was time to study them in class, it seemed more like a review and the homework and studying would go more quickly. Robin had also decided to sign up for the sailing lessons at the Buckelsmere Town Park that were offered for two weeks in August. Ann knew it wasn't so much an interest in sailing as it might be an interest in the young instructors in white shorts and navy polo shirts with whistles, and that Caela had also signed up. It would pass the time. Next summer

Robin would be allowed to get her working papers and hopefully find a summer job, even if only part time. She had a lead on a packing job at a local cookie cutter factory through a friend, Angel Lopez, whom she knew from her high school select choir. He was already working there this summer as he was a year older.

    Bill looked at the GPS on the Jeep's dashboard. It said the trip would be 99 miles and take about two hours. It was early. They hoped that by leaving so early, it had saved them at least an hour in dreaded shore traffic, even though it was a weekday and there still could be a lot of traffic. Bill knew he could always nap after lunch if he thought he needed it, but the excitement of being under the same roof with Suzanne for a week would probably prove to cure any need for sleep on his part.

    Bill thought back to when he had met her last December in the rehabilitation center after Ann's broken hip accident. He smiled to himself. He liked Suzanne, really liked her. They had gone out to dinner a couple of times, and had attended an art exhibition in Doylestown, the county seat not far away from Buckelsmere. He had taken her down into Philadelphia to a matinee reprisal of "Oklahoma" when he had learned she enjoyed Rodgers and Hammerstein musicals. Afterwards they had dinner in a small French bistro that he had frequented over the three years he had lived in the city and worked with Ann as a junior detective. Suzanne had reciprocated by inviting him to her home for Easter dinner in April. On paper it would appear their relationship was moving forward, even if very slowly, but Bill knew he should not rush Suzanne. She had spent fifteen years as a very independent widow, and he did not want to scare her off by being too aggressive. This week together – worrisome, yet wonderful!

    After Ann's accident, and her leaving the Philadelphia Police Department last December, Bill had taken the Detective position at the Buckelsmere Police Department at her encouragement. But it didn't take anyone twisting his arm. Bill had been so very ready to change jobs that the offer from the Buckelsmere police force seemed too good to be true.

One of the best things about the move was he was now head of the department's detectives with only a Detective Corporal below him, and the Chief of Police and Lieutenant above him in rank. Working in Buckelsmere had proved a big change from working in the huge Philadelphia Police Force with its layers and layers of titles and levels of positions. Bill found the work here in Buckelsmere steady, but luckily it wasn't a 24-7 type of detective job.

There was free time – time to think and relax, and *write*. He'd been burnt out after three years on the Philadelphia Police force, with little energy or inspiration left for his writing. Now he was coming alive again with plot and characters popping into his head constantly. His detective stories continued to be popular in the *Black Mask Magazine* and this week he had heard that his first full length novel had been accepted by a very prestigious publishing house in New York City. It was all coming together at last. Writing was his passion; detective work paid the bills.

He'd take this week off completely – no police work, no writing. He had decided to use the week to decompress, relax and recharge. And to work on his relationship with Suzanne. He hoped she would still be interested in him after having him underfoot for a whole week.

The two teens had fallen asleep for most of the ride. When the Jeep left the Garden State Parkway, Robin and Caela stirred, happy to realize how close they were to their Beach Week! They had talked and planned it all out once they knew they were going and that Caela was welcomed along as well.

Plenty of bedrooms, Suzanne had said. Robin couldn't wait to have Caela there to explore the beach, the boardwalk, the boys! The lifeguards, specifically. What a dream! Robin thought.

"How much farther?" Ann asked.

"A quick stop right up here at the wine store, then about ten minutes tops," John answered.

"I'll go in with you," Bill offered, thinking a few bottles of sparkling Italian wine would make a nice treat. He reminded himself that he should send a few postcards in the next day or so. He always tried to send one to his mom, favorite sister, and to his three great-aunts, so he'd look for the postcards until he found some. He'd not been to Ocean City, New Jersey before. Once during his three years on the Philadelphia Police Department, he'd gone with some of the men to Atlantic City for the boxing matches held at one of the large casinos. He found the whole thing too dirty, too sleazy, too depressing. Not his style. Bill hoped the simple combination of sun and sand and Suzanne would restore his perception of what the New Jersey coast should be.

Caela wanted to talk with Robin about how soon they could reasonably get to the beach; how far the beach was from Suzanne's house; how much adult supervision would there likely be while they were on the beach. She had already turned fourteen and was feeling pretty grown up and independent. When Robin relayed that there would be lifeguards every few hundred feet down the beach all day long, it had been all Caela could think about for weeks leading up to the trip. Because she knew the Essexes well, and now was fairly familiar with Suzanne and Bill, she knew that the time they spent at the house would be interesting if not very exciting. Suzanne had promised excursions on the days that dawned unsuitable for the beach, a party next door with friends and neighbors, the 4th July Baby Parade, fireworks, and of course the evening strolls on the boardwalk for treats, games and rides. Caela's mom had slipped her an extra twenty dollars just as she was leaving their house the night before to stay over with Robin for the early morning start. Caela wondered what her mom would think if she found out that her dad had also given her an extra twenty-dollar bill for the week – just in case! Hopefully neither would find out what the other had done, and neither would ask her for an accounting on where their twenty dollars had gone.

The men returned and stowed the wine in the back with all of their suitcases. One Suitcase Each! Ann had told each of them. This took John a little time shifting things around to get everything in and secure again. Then it was only a short ride over the causeway, over the Bay, and onto the barrier island into downtown Ocean City.

John carefully negotiated his way up to Suzanne's street, then turned right, towards the ocean as she was on the block closest to the ocean, beach and boardwalk. He pulled the Jeep into her driveway at Diamond Dunes, and came to a stop.

Chapter 2

The Same Day July 2

It was a large gray and white house, with nautical blue awnings to block out the heat of the afternoon sun, built on pilings to raise it up a story, out of the reach of storm or flooding on the ground level. Underneath the house, there was parking for four cars, a storage area and the outdoor showers.

John pulled his Jeep up behind Suzanne's car, leaving room for others, just in case. As the five of them piled out of the car onto the concrete parking pad, Suzanne came through a door that led up a staircase to the living areas of the house. All smiles upon seeing them, Suzanne waved a hello. She was wearing a sunflower patterned sundress and flip-flops, the ubiquitous footwear of the shore.

"Welcome! Welcome!" Suzanne said amidst quick hugs and a melee of everyone grabbing their own bags, food items, and the wine out of the back of the Jeep. It would take two trips to get everything upstairs.

"Come upstairs, and we'll get all this sorted. What? What's this," Suzanne said, pulling a note off the outside of the door leading to the staircase. She read it aloud, "Warning, Residents! OCPD wants everyone to be vigilant as there has been a series of break-ins and robberies. Please be sure to secure all valuables and keep your doors and windows locked when you are not at home."

"Oh great, just what we all needed – crime and police work here at the shore. Thought you had escaped it, I bet!" Suzanne laughed. "No worries, we lock this door when we leave. I will tell all of you the four-digit code to get in, so you can all come and go without my having to hand out keys to everyone," Suzanne explained, pointing at the keypad lock on the door.

Bill nervously looked at Suzanne. He didn't want to get off on the wrong foot. Suzanne glanced in his direction several times before catching his eye, and when she did, she smiled at him, only him, even though she was talking to the whole group.

"Welcome to Diamond Dunes, your beach house for the next week. Consider it your home during this time. Come and go as you please, do as much or as little as you want. I will let you know of any group activities in advance, as soon as I know about them. The only thing so far is that on the 4th of July, our street has a Baby and Bike Parade at 6:00 p.m. for all the children, and then after that we have been invited next door," Suzanne inclined her head to the house next door, one house closer to the beach, "for a barbeque following the parade. Mike and Wendy always have a bunch of people for supper and to stay for the fireworks. Wendy's barbecued ribs are to die for!"

Caela looked at the house next door, just as a young man in his late teens, came out of the house and waved at Suzanne and her guests and headed toward the beach. He was wearing the orange-red bathing suit and tank top of a lifeguard. Caela turned, smiled and nodded at Robin, who nodded her head and smiled in return.

Suzanne noticed the silent communication. "That's Al, the son next door. He is a lifeguard this summer before he heads off to college in late August," she said as she raised her hand in a wave to Al.

"Now, let's grab all this stuff, although it looks like several trips, doesn't it, and get it upstairs."

"I did tell them all – one suitcase!" Ann said, "but with the stop for wine, and the lasagna dinner, we did fill up the Jeep, didn't we?"

"No worries," Bill said, "I'll come back down for whatever is left."

Suzanne continued, "The house was built in the 1950's by Frank's dad, Aldo Beck. It was built on pilings to keep it up out of any flooding due to tides or storms. It has worked well so far – 60 some years. They say later in the week we may have the double whammy of a full moon and a storm moving in, pushing the tides very high so we may get street flooding. We'll see. It never lasts long.

"There are two outdoor showers for when we return from the beach. There is nothing more exhilarating than showering outdoors with the air loose and free around your legs and head. If you haven't done it before, you are in for a real treat. I'd put an outdoor shower in my home back in Buckelsmere, but the town fathers and the zoning board probably wouldn't approve of it. You bring your showering stuff and change of clothes down before you head to the beach and leave it all in the cubby holes marked by the bedroom – you'll see. Frank's dad thought it all out pretty well.

"Over here in the storage area there are beach chairs, umbrellas, and water toys if you would enjoy those. And there is a clothesline at the back where we hang up the beach towels and bathing suits to dry. Before you head upstairs, flip flops off, and a quick step into the washbasin of water to get the last of the sand off your feet. This door with the combination lock heads up to the living area. This week the code will be 1-1-1-2. I post it on a dry erase board right here in the staircase in case you need to see it again before you leave and close the door behind you."

"Let me guess – your birthday?" John asked.

Suzanne blushed. "Too simple?"

"From a security point of view, if it were the internet, probably. But here at the shore, I'm not sure anyone would guess it randomly," Ann responded.

Bill made a mental note of her birthday and circled it in red on his mind's calendar. He hadn't thought of when her birthday might be, and was heartily glad he had not missed it these last few months. Maybe Ann or John would have given him the heads up in advance, but now that he knew, he'd be prepared. November. Four months. Ages to plan and prepare.

Suzanne pushed the keys on the touch pad, which buzzed slightly and she opened the door.

"There's a brick there," she said pointing at a gray brick with a seagull painted on it. "In case you need to prop the door open to carry groceries or things up. Like now. Robin, push the door open all the way and put that brick against the bottom of it for now. We'll be back down soon enough, headed to the beach – I am so glad you arrived early enough for a swim this morning. Let's change into our bathing suits. We'll lock up when we head to the beach," Suzanne explained. Everyone grabbed an armful and headed up the enclosed staircase to the next level. There was another door, unlocked, which Suzanne went through into a large kitchen/dining room/living room, stretching out with a large deck at the back of the living area. Truly a great room.

"Ann, you and John will have the suite on this floor. It'll save your going up and down another flight of stairs. I know the hip is much better, but no sense aggravating it. John, you go left here, toward the front of the house. If the breezes are good, it is a delight to open the sliding door to the private deck, and let the breezes blow through. Drop your bags and join us for the rest of the tour."

When John returned a minute later, Suzanne continued her explanation of where everyone would be sleeping. "This is our main entertainment area here – kitchen, large dining table off to the side here, big enough for all that will be here this week, I'm sure. The living room faces the back of the house, no real view, but quieter and with great access to the deck out back. Not much to look at – just the backs of the houses across the alley, but more outside area and a way to open the house up when it's not too hot."

"You said Frank's dad built this?" Bill asked.

"Yes, Aldo came into some money in the 1950's. He sold a restaurant or something, bought and moved the family into the Buckelsmere house where I still live, and built this house for family vacations. Frank was an only child, so no telling why Frank's dad thought he needed a shore house with five bedrooms. I kept it all . . ." Suzanne trailed off, suddenly deep in thought, a world and an age ago.

"Well, I just love it," John said, trying to bring back Suzanne's happier mood. She smiled at him. She knew that sometimes her sorrow over the past seemed to overwhelm her. Her husband Frank was killed fifteen years ago in Iraq, and she had lived alone since.

Bill took a look around as Suzanne and the others headed to the staircase to continue up to the next level. He saw the big country style kitchen, with all the modern conveniences. Suzanne must have put in the white cabinets with newer granite countertops more recently. The dining room area had a long table with eight chairs. Frank's dad had probably brought a lot of the furniture down to the shore house when he built it. Sturdy and serviceable, even if it was terribly outdated. There were extra chairs in the corner of the room, no doubt for when leaves were put into the table extending it to seat at least twelve.

The living room had a variety of couch seating and wicker chairs with floral cushions. Bill noticed the house was cooler than outdoors already even at 9:30 a.m. so Suzanne have had central air installed at some point. There was a game/card table in one corner, a bookcase loaded with books and board games, and a box of sporting equipment from a bygone era. A sisal rug lay underfoot, not comfy on the feet, but better against the sand inevitably tracked in. It would be fun to be here with Suzanne and the group in the evenings, Bill thought. Then he turned and followed the group already ahead of him going up the staircase to the next level.

Suzanne was pointing toward the front of the house. "There is a small nook up front and a door to a balcony overlooking the street. Off that part of the hallway is another small hallway leading to three bedrooms – CheChe is in the one to the right and Bill will be in the room straight ahead on the side of the house. You two girls will be in the room to the left in the front of the house, as it has twin beds, and you will use the hall bathroom. My room is in the back of the house. Drop your bags off in your rooms, as there is more to explore."

Suzanne started towards the staircase again, and headed up, knowing the others would follow. When she reached the roof deck level, she opened another locked door and stepped out into the sun. The breeze in her short black hair, seagulls calling overhead, the blue of the sea off to the east, the surrounding neighborhood on all sides – magnificent. It was a large area, easily twenty-five feet square. Cushioned seating was built in on all sides. A couple of tables were folded down and stowed with bungie cords against the staircase wall; no doubt to prevent them from being carried off by the wind. There were the appropriate and expected oohs and aahs over the magnificent views and expansive party space.

"Cocktails at sunset!" Suzanne said succinctly. Bill nodded, glad he had brought the cheese balls and veggies. He knew he'd have a hard time waiting for that time of the day.

"Let's change into our swimsuits. Bill, if you could fetch whatever we left down below, it would be a help. Then everyone go back down to the street level when you are ready. I have the beach tags for everyone. You will find each bedroom has a unique color scheme – yellow, blue, green, pink – with all the bath towels and beach towels matching the color scheme of your room so you can easily tell which ones are yours. Also bring your clothes down to put on after showering. We leave all those downstairs in the matching cubbies at the outdoor showers for après beach, so to speak.

"Che-Che should be back any minute. She ran to the store for additional food supplies for me. I knew we'd need a big green salad for tonight, and I wanted fresh cold cuts and cheese for lunch later. House Rule – everyone gets their own breakfast - cereal, toast, donuts, whatever. Everyone helps themselves to luncheon supplies – sandwich fixings, anything leftover in the fridge. We've already assigned dinners to Ann, Che-Che, John and Bill, a BBQ next door so we'll decide on any other dinners as we reach them – we can eat leftovers, place a take-out order or go to a local place for a seafood or pasta dinner.

"There's a lovely sea breeze today. Cool air off the ocean. Let's hope that lasts all week. If we get a west wind, a land breeze, we'll be fighting off the biting flies on the beach and sometimes even up on the roof deck. We can sit out in the screened porch, but let's all hope for sea breezes."

"Why did Frank's dad name the house Diamond Dunes?" Bill asked.

"Well, 'Dunes' obviously for the sand dunes near the beach. There are some there still and they are well protected, but mostly now they are under the boardwalk area. 'Diamond' I am not too sure about, but it has a nice ring to it, 'Diamond Dunes'. Most of the houses have clever names. You'll see 'Dad's Retreat', 'Beachy Keen', 'Sea Duced', 'Beach Haven', 'Aqua Vista'. Some people are so clever how they work their names into the name like 'Barnacle Bill's' or 'Moore Relaxing'. I kept the house name, along with everything else as you have noticed. I did upgrade the kitchen, for what little cooking I do! I replaced all the mattresses, and repainted the interior in soft beach colors. I like to think it all looks like a roll of Necco Wafers!"

Once again on the living level, they found Suzanne's friend, Che-Che, had arrived back from a quick morning trip to the grocery store. She was stowing fruit, veggies, milk and cold cuts into the refrigerator. Bread, rolls, and chips she left on the island for later.

Suzanne started the introductions, "Che-Che, you remember John and Ann, daughter Robin, and Robin's friend, Caela. And this is Buckelsmere's finest, Detective Bill Dancer." Bill felt the blush rising to his dimples. Suzanne was teasing him a bit, but he decided that was okay, as long as she was glad that he was here. Bill turned and studied Che-Che.

Suzanne continued, "Che-Che's real name is Florencia Rosita Maria Reyes, but I call her Che-Che as she is a dear friend that I hope you all will also call your dear friend by week's end." Che-Che was dark haired, and darker complexioned than Suzanne or Anne. That could just be that she tanned more easily, Bill thought. Medium tall, but built like a mature lady super hero – curves and well-defined muscles. This woman looked like a spokesperson for Tae Bo, or a karate school. Bill decided he wanted her on his team if it ever came to a fight. She had quick eyes, and a flashy smile that spoke to her intelligence and good humor. Bill could immediately see how Suzanne would find her fun to be around.

Bill recalled having heard Suzanne speak about Che-Che. "D.A.R.?" he asked.

"Yes," Che-Che said, "Suzanne and I are both in the same Chapter. We hope to be able to finish up any research that Ann needs so we can send her application in."

"Here's hoping!" Ann said. "I did bring some notes along, just in case we have some down time and can fit it in."

"I have my laptop," Che-Che said. "I'm sure we will have some evening hours, or perhaps some time if it rains."

Caela pulled on Robin's sleeve, bringing Robin back to their mission for the day.

"Beach time, you said, Suzanne?" Robin asked, trying to speed up the casual talk.

"Yes, yes, of course. Everyone, make sure you have your towels and sunblock, and let's get going."

Chapter 3

That Same Morning, July 2

They had all changed into their bathing suits and coverups; gathered up their sunblock, hats, & chairs from the storage locker and deposited their bath towels and clothes into their color-coded showering cubbyholes. Then, the laughing, happy group started down the sidewalk for the one block walk to the beach. They passed other large beach houses with colorful awnings, screened porches, seashell and stone front yards, and the sounds of children playing and getting ready for their day.

When they reached the end of the block, there was a set of wood stairs from the street level up to the boardwalk. Brown's Donuts was to their left. Suzanne pointed it out to them in case anyone felt the need to stand in line for an hour or so to buy donuts. Then they passed through the morning's bike traffic on the boardwalk, and walked the short distance down the sand to where the lifeguard's stand was located. Once on duty, as they were at this point of the day, the lifeguards would have put up flags designating the safe swimming area that they watched over.

Suzanne waved hello to a group of people down the beach a bit who waved back. Suzanne explained, "My next-door neighbors, Mike and Wendy, and it looks like their married daughter, Kathy, her husband, Stephen, and adorable little one, Jack. The others must be Stephen's family. Mike did say they'd be coming this week at some point for the 4th of July. After we get settled, I will take you down and introduce you all," Suzanne said, dropping her beach bag and starting to set up her chair.

"Here's good. We want to stay above the high tide mark. Tide's coming in, I checked the tide chart which I keep posted in the kitchen on the fridge. High tide today is about noon." Suzanne smiled as she watched Robin and Caela position their beach towels on the sand as close to the lifeguard stand as they could. Suzanne knew Al from next door was a lifeguard this summer, but wasn't sure which stand he was currently on, as they were rotated around during the day. She supposed that helped them stay 'fresh' and no one lifeguard had an easier assignment than any other lifeguard.

Ann and John walked to the water's edge and waded in. Ann said it wasn't cold; John said it was too cold. Ann knew the water temperature to be between 65 and 70 degrees at this point in the summer. Ann held onto John's beach shirt as she waded out into the water, as the sun's brightness made it difficult for her to see very well; her eyes had become very light sensitive in recent years. Ann was determined to get wet, and she waded into the water until it was mid-calf on her legs to let the waves wash by her. John had walked back up to stand in the shallower water. Ann would have to fend for herself if a large or unusually strong wave came toward her.

Che-Che slipped off her coverup and strode down to the water's edge and straight out into the water without any hesitation, diving under a breaking wave when she was out far enough. She was a competent and brave swimmer, with a smooth gliding action as she swam back and forth in front of the lifeguard's stand for the exercise of it. When she finally did come out, she shook her head, the sea water spraying off her shoulder-length dark brown hair cascading a giant rainbow of droplets in the mid-day sun.

Bill sat in his chair. His bathing suit and beach shirt conspicuous in their newness. He wasn't historically a beach person, having grown up on the family farm west of Harrisburg. And he was white. He knew it and somehow was embarrassed suddenly. Stupid, he said to himself. Stupid not to get a pre-beach tan at home over the last couple of weeks. But, also stupid to feel this way. Half of the people on the beach were as white as he was.

"Shall I spray some sunblock on your back?" Suzanne asked him, stirring him from his reverie.

"Yes, please. I guess you'd better," Bill answered dropping his shirt and letting Suzanne spray him. The cold spray covered his strong back. Bill felt naked in only his swim trunks. But he yanked himself back from that thought and generously offered to spray Suzanne's back. Perhaps that is why she had offered to do his back – she wanted him to do hers. Once coated, Suzanne put on her big red sunhat to protect her black hair and face from the sun, waved down to John and Ann at the water's edge. John waved back; Ann hadn't seen her wave. Suzanne sat down in her chair next to Bill, thinking him quite a bit more handsome and better built than those skinny lifeguard boys that Robin and Caela were so intently studying.

"Not much of a beach person?" Suzanne asked.

"Not much experience. I don't dislike the beach; I just have never spend much time at the beach. I just need to get used to it."

Suzanne wore big dark sunglasses as well. Bill thought there was a bit of Sophia Loren about her with her black hair, large hat and oversized dark sunglasses. Glamorous.

"Why are you smiling?" Suzanne asked, a bit of suspicion on her face. Bill laughed; he hadn't realized he was smiling. That made him smile even more.

"I was thinking how glamorous you look. Very movie star-ish, if that is a word," Bill said.

Suzanne laughed, partly in disbelief, partly in embarrassment. "You'll do well to remember that some morning when you see me just out of the shower with wet hair and no makeup."

"I relish the thought," Bill said, then realized too late it might make him appear too forward and too invasive. God, what was he thinking! But Suzanne took no notice, or at least showed no offence to his statement.

"I have everyone's beach tags here if the attendant should come around and check. I keep them in a zipper bag so we don't lose them in the surf or sand. I've actually seen the seagulls pick them up off of beach towels and out of the sand and fly away with them. I can only imagine a huge pile of beach tags somewhere – somewhere perhaps where the seagulls go at nighttime, a nest of beach tags," Suzanne said.

"We normally stay until lunchtime," Suzanne explained, glancing over at Robin and Caela on their beach towels talking up to the lifeguards on their stand. "I do hope they lathered up with sun block. They don't need to be ill with sun poisoning after only their first day. Kids."

"You like kids?" Bill ventured. Something that had never come up before between them. He tried to appear casual, distracted, or as if he was just following her lead in the conversation.

"Yes, I guess. I don't have any myself, as you know. But I suppose I am not totally opposed to the idea of children," Suzanne said and then paused. Should she continue, or leave it there? Should she speak totally openly this soon? She had set up this whole house party so that she could invite Bill and have him around for the whole week without it looking too obvious. She knew in her heart she wanted to get to know him better, but to do that, she was going to have to open up about herself as well. How to proceed forward, Suzanne wondered?

"I'm forty-one," she decided would suffice.

"I know," Bill said, then noticing her surprise added, "I'm a detective, remember," and smiled at her. Bill knew that more smiling and less babbling might win the day. "I'm thirty-three."

"I know. My best friend, Ann, is a detective remember. I suppose I would want children . . . although time is passing . . ."

"Yes, me, too," Bill said, finishing the awkwardness.

Che-Che returned from her long and vigorous swim at that point, dripping seawater on both of them and flopped herself into her chair, giving both Suzanne and Bill the excuse to drop their conversation.

"The ocean is lovely today. Warm, I say. Really warm. Bill, you *must* get in, get wet. No one should be allowed lunch if their bathing suit is dry!"

"Okay, maybe it is time. I will try at least. I can't promise much as I am not much of a swimmer," Bill said as he rose and started to walk to the water's edge, where John and Ann still stood in the water, talking and holding hands.

When Bill was out of earshot Che-Che turned to Suzanne. "And . . . "

"And . . . what?"

"How is the romance going?"

"Che-Che! I am shocked! There's no romance – "

"– Yet –"

"– Yet – Okay, yet. I admit I find this man very attractive. And because of John and Ann knowing and trusting him, I can assume he has no baggage to bring along, nor any skeletons in his closet or they would have warned me already. As he seems a decent, honest, hardworking man, I was able to skip right over some of the objections I normally have. But, Che-Che, he's younger. Eight years younger."

"Does it matter? He's a grownup. You're a grownup. Statistically, it might be better – you'll have each other into your old age. His being younger will never change how old you are. You'll never be younger. He is very attractive; I'll give you that." Che-Che watched Bill as he walked into the water, his muscled shoulders and trim waistline in contrast with many of the other men on the beach who did not work at keeping as fit as Bill obviously did. "He has a good job. He seems reasonable. You probably are wise to try out the co-habitation aspect this week with all of us around as a buffer. Let's see what, if any, horrible personal habits he has. Let's just see if they are insurmountable."

"Yes, that was my plan. Let's just see. No decisions need to be made right now. Let's just see if he can get through this week with passing marks," Suzanne said, at ease confiding in her good friend.

The Diamond Dunes Murders

Bill walked to the water and stuck his feet in. Colder than he would have liked it. As he stood there, the waves came in and brushed past his legs, some even as high as his knees. He started to get used to the water and it didn't seem as cold. He turned his back to the ocean and looked up the beach toward where Suzanne sat talking with Che-Che. Robin and Caela were off to his right, nearer the lifeguard stand. Of course. That Caela! She'd either become real trouble, or she'd start to even out and mature a bit. But right now, at fourteen, Caela was more than he wanted to deal with. Ann and John seemed okay with her, so he would follow their lead on the situation. Kids!

Kids! Now that was a question Bill had not expected to have to tackle so soon. He knew he liked kids. He knew he'd like to have a family himself, but if he decided to try with Suzanne, it might be difficult or perhaps even impossible. Did he want to risk that, face that possibility?

Too soon to decide. He'd see how this thing with Suzanne progressed. She'd be forty-two in November. He promised himself he'd decide before then – go forward or back off completely. He needed to be fair to her as well as fair to himself. He could hear his mother's and sisters' objections already. He'd have to have all his ducks in a row before he said too much to the family. Maybe they would just be happy for him, no matter what he decided. Yes, November.

In the heat of the rising noon sun, the spray of the salt water at each crashing wave around him, and the sound of children's laughter along the shore line, Bill felt November was luckily a long way off, giving him ample time to establish where he and Suzanne would end up.

Bill watched the people on the beach, watched the seagulls coming and going, hoping for a French fry or scrap of anything left by the bathers. He could see only as far west as the boardwalk, as the shops and amusements that ran the length of the beach were tall enough to hide everything beyond. Further south there appeared to be a Ferris wheel on the boardwalk and a pier that extended out into the ocean. Perhaps a fishing pier, or an amusement pier of some kind. To the north, he could see the casino towers in Atlantic City through the rising haze.

Suzanne had mentioned that they normally went to the boardwalk an evening or two after dinner when it was cooler. He made a mental note to look for postcards to send home, and pick up some salt water taffy for his mom and great aunts. Earlier that day, when he had been changing into his bathing suit, he had quickly looked through a brochure of ads for local businesses and events that Suzanne had left in his room. He had noticed there were coupons in the brochure, so he'd be sure to take them along with him when they did go.

There were beach walkers, shell collectors, and joggers going in both directions. There was a man with a metal detector as well. Bill watched as he crisscrossed the sand, searching for coins or jewelry. Bill wondered if the man found enough treasure to be able to not hold a day job. Or perhaps this guy was just here for the week, visiting, like himself. The detectorist would walk in a W pattern up and down the beach, keeping the head of his metal detector fairly close to the sand, hoping to hear the beeps in his headset. When he did, he'd scoop up some sand in his long-armed sieve, shake out the sand and hope for treasure. More often than not, Bill knew it would only be a coin or bottle cap. But there was the possibility it could be someone's lost diamond ring or a long forgotten Spanish doubloon washed up from the depths of the ocean.

It was relaxing, or tiring, Bill couldn't decide which. The pull of the waves on his legs, the bright sunshine baking his back, the constant happy sounds of children playing. He walked out of the water and back up the beach.

Ann spoke to him. "Had enough, Bill?"

"For now, but it is lovely, I must admit. I'm not much of a swimmer, so I guess I am just being initially cautious, until I get used to it. Then I might surprise myself."

"In a little while we'll head back to the house for a shower and then lunch. I find that the beach gets too hot to spend the whole day here," Ann explained.

John nodded in agreement. "Yes, and then there's a bit of time for a short nap on the back porch before cocktails and Ann's lasagna dinner tonight."

"Sounds wonderful," Bill said, his eyes on Suzanne, who was approaching them.

"Hey," she said.

"Hey, yourself," Ann replied, "You going in?"

"I think not. I'll just feel it with my toes and keep my hair intact today. Tomorrow will be soon enough for me."

"Well, I'm going to risk getting wet, to say I did so, so here goes," Ann said and took a couple of steps out into the water. John followed, looking unsure that he wanted to join her, but deciding he better be there for backup. Ann's hip had healed, but she often said she felt it was 'weak' and a bit painful at times. John didn't want to have to rescue Ann if a wave should knock her down and start to drag her out to sea. So, he'd stay close.

Robin and Caela arrived at that point, too, and plunged in alongside Ann, unafraid, unhindered, and squealing that the sea was cold and *not* warm as Che-Che had assured them. After twenty minutes or so, they all returned together to the shallow water to stand with Bill and Suzanne.

"Do you feel like lunch?" Suzanne asked them.

"Yes, please! We're starving. Breakfast seems like ages ago," Robin exclaimed.

They all gathered up their towels and chairs, slipped their still sandy feet into their flip-flops for the walk up the now blazingly hot sand to the boardwalk to cross over and down to street level. The early morning bikers had been replaced by walkers and shoppers, some still in their bathing suits, searching for a slice of pizza or perhaps a pork roll sandwich. Suzanne led the happy, hot, sandy, wet group down the stairs on the street side of the boardwalk and the short one block walk back to Diamond Dunes.

The sun, the sand, the blue waves rolling in to crash in frothy white, the laughing children and calling gulls – it all belied plans already put into motion that would turn their vacation week upside down, and change all of their lives.

Chapter 4

Afternoon, July 2

Ann walked carefully so she would not trip over an uneven edge of the sidewalk; the others walked on ahead at their own pace, just a bit faster than she and John who had hung back with her.

Maybe it was that the day had already been long, or maybe it was the hour that she had stood in the sun and surf with the water dragging and pushing at her legs. Maybe it was that she was hungry and a bit dehydrated, but Ann was starting to hear a familiar hum, a soft thin thread of sound, of music almost; not a cry, not words, but something. Something causing her to feel apprehensive and unsettled. Was it the siren of the seas? She'd heard of such things. Was it the merfolk trying to communicate? Ann knew she was being fanciful. Merfolk! She knew she had heard it before, had felt it before, long ago and several times since. Times she had tried hard to ignore and deny. But it was there in her head. The soft hum. The soft hum that she did not talk about.

"John, when we get back to Suzanne's would you rinse your feet off and run upstairs to fetch me an iced tea with double sugar. I'm feeling like I really need it."

"Sure, no problem. You get in line for the shower, and I will get you something to revive you. Then we'll be upstairs for lunch before you know it," John agreed, alarmed that Ann was starting to feel poorly, hoping that not having eaten recently was all it was. John knew sometimes Ann felt a little peckish if it had been a while since she had eaten.

John was glad he could see Diamond Dune's nautical blue awnings only a few houses away. They were getting close. And as they approached the house at street level, they came up behind the rest of their group that had all stopped together on the sidewalk, silent.

Sitting on the outside steps that lead up to front deck off the living level from the sidewalk, sat a woman. Petite, dark haired, brightly dressed, sporting an eye-patch over her left eye, with a sheet of paper in her hand.

When this woman realized the group standing on the sidewalk were the residents of Diamond Dunes, she stood up, stepped down to the sidewalk and uttered a loud "Cousin Suzanne!" and opened her arms in an attempt to initiate a hug. Suzanne stepped forward one cautious step.

"And you are?"

"Cousin Catarina Blackpaw! I'm Frank's cousin, Catarina, from Maine. I was in the area and thought I'd stop in and say hello," the woman said, advancing towards Suzanne, and giving her a somewhat distant, huggy-kissy greeting, so as to not get wet or sandy.

Robin stood behind Ann, not hiding exactly, but the intrusion of such an odd character had left her unsure what to do. She'd take her cue from her mother. 'Cousin Catarina?' Robin thought. 'Blackpaw?!?' Robin questioned in her own mind. Robin didn't know anyone from Maine, just that it was east and north, way up there, that there were moose and lobsters, but that was about all that she did know. Perhaps all people from Maine were short, dark people with bright hot pink and orange short sets, and eye patches.

"Forgive me, Catarina, it's been so long, I didn't recognize you," Suzanne said when she had gathered herself once again. "These are my very good friends, Ann, daughter Robin, husband John, and friends Caela, Che-Che and Bill. Maybe you have time for a sandwich with us?" Suzanne said, being a generous hostess to a long forgotten relative of her late husband.

"Lunch? But of course, and maybe you'd put me up for a few days, no? Anywhere, it doesn't matter. It is just so very, very nice to be here to see you," and with that Catarina turned, picked up a small duffle bag sitting at the bottom of the stairs and waited with a smile for her invitation.

"Oh, and the police stopped by. They were handing out these leaflets. Seems there has been a spate of break-ins and robberies. They want everyone to be vigilant," Catarina said, passing the paper over to Suzanne.

"Yes, we have seen that. They stuck one in the door earlier. We shower down here first, then go up the center staircase. This way," Suzanne said to Catarina, who fell in with the pack of friends and headed underneath the house to the outside showers and changing area.

Ann's nerves were prickling with alarm; She knew she should take her cue from Suzanne who obviously knew this woman, but there was something off about the whole thing. The humming she heard on the walk down the block from the beach, the mermadic melody, had intensified. Surely there was a logical and acceptable explanation for this woman's sudden, unexpected arrival. Ann needed a cold drink, some lunch, and a quiet moment with Suzanne. She hoped that would relieve this warning buzz in her head.

Shortly after that, John returned to her side with the sweet iced tea, encouraging her to drink up and solve her flutters. The seven of them took their turns showering and dressing quickly in shorts and tee-shirts, ascending the stairs to the open living room – kitchen area. Catarina stood quiet as the others joined her at the kitchen island.

"What do you want to do?" Ann had asked Suzanne quietly when they were coming up the staircase.

"I don't know. Seems impertinent for her to just show up and expect not only that I would be here but that there would be room for her. But Frank did have a cousin Catarina in Maine. He used to visit her and her family there during the summers as a child, I believe. It's been so long since I was with any of Frank's family – I just don't know – I – "

"Understood. Put her on an uncomfortable roll away cot, in a corner somewhere. Maybe she'll take the hint and leave tomorrow. That way you won't have to be rude to her and ask her to leave," Ann suggested.

"Yes. You are right. At least it's a better plan than I have come up with at this minute. I'll put it in the front nook down the hallway by the girls' and Bill's door. She'll have to share the hall bathroom with Robin and Caela. That in itself ought to be the incentive to move along. I'll get Bill to help me move it and set it up. You and Che-Che, if you would, could you lay out the tray of cold cuts and cheese, and condiments from the refrigerator? Bread, rolls and chips are out on the island. Cookies are on top of the refrigerator. Paper plates and cups in the island cabinet nearest the stove top."

Suzanne turned to Bill, "Bill, could you help me a minute?" Then to Catarina she said, "Catarina, as you see we have a full house but we could squeeze you in for a day or so. We'll set up a cot in the hallway and you can share the bathroom with Caela and Robin. I'm sure you won't mind – for a day or so."

Catarina bristled. Ann could tell by the look on her face and her jerky movements that a roll away cot in what was actually just a hallway and sharing a bathroom with two teenagers was NOT what she expected nor was her due as a 'relation.' Oh my, Ann thought, things could get interesting now.

During the heat of the afternoon, and after their sandwich lunch was cleaned up and everything put away, the group found quiet things with which to pass the time. Bill decided to sit out on the screened in porch with John, both achieving a nap for an hour or so in the quiet warm breeze. Robin and Caela worked on a jigsaw puzzle on the gaming table while they played some music on the CD player nearby. Occasionally they would start singing along, unaware they were doing it, eventually drifting off into silence again. Ann and Suzanne sat with Che-Che at the dining room table. Che-Che worked at the laptop with her ancestor research paperwork that she had brought along.

"Say, Che-Che, how are you coming on your Supplemental Patriot?" Suzanne asked.

"Not too badly. It's just a matter of time . . . finding all the birth, marriage and death records. I'm pretty close now. He's such an interesting Patriot, I can't wait to list him as one of mine."

Ann could see Catarina was at a loss about what they were discussing.

"Patriot?" Catarina said, wandering over to the table from the kitchen stool where she had parked herself.

"Yes, if you have an ancestor who fought in the Revolutionary War or contributed somehow, like paying a tax or contributing goods to the army, and if you can prove your lineage back to that person, you can apply to be a member of the Daughters of the American Revolution."

Che-Che could see Catarina was not impressed nor cared.

"Che-Che is already a member, but she is working on what we call a Supplemental – another Patriot in her family tree. It takes the same about of work, but this one is especially interesting as he was a Spaniard who aided the Colonials in the fight against England.

There was an even blanker look on Catarina's face. Suzanne decided to take a different approach to including her in-law cousin in the conversation.

"Isn't it just so interesting that we have such a diverse group here at Diamond Dunes! Che-Che and her people came from Cuba and immigrated to Louisiana originally, then to Pennsylvania in the 1930's to work in the Bethlehem steel mills. John and Ann are from English and Scottish descent. Caela is very Irish if I might say so," Caela looked up and smiled, "Bill – gee, I don't know about Bill. You, of course, are of Native American, English, Dutch and Italian descent," Suzanne said.

Catarina's eyes twitched. Just ever so slightly. Ann caught it, even with her own poor vision as they were sitting fairly close to each other. A twitch of nerves? A twitch, a tell. Catarina did not know her own heritage, but how could she not know? A twitch of alarm? Ann was not sure, but she did know this was significant. Just that eye twitch. Ann had seen the same twitch a hundred times in suspects when confronted with the facts in a crime that they had hoped would remain undiscovered. Ann's professional experience told her to note this well.

Che-Che picked up the thread. "My people came from Cuba so many years ago to the Louisiana area, where we lived and fished, and prospered. Eventually my grandfather thought he'd do better to come north during the Great Depression and work in the steel mills. He was Cuban yes, but spoke both fluent English and Spanish. He was a huge help to the mill supervisors as he could translate for both them and the Spanish speaking workers. It was hard times then, yet not bad times. My father remembers playing with the other children and it seemed an adventure to him.

"Since Suzanne mentioned it, my Revolutionary War Patriot that I am trying to prove as an ancestor is Juan de Miralles, born in Spain and died of fever in George Washington's camp in Morristown, New Jersey in 1780. Juan acted as an observer of the Continental Army for the Spanish, first in Philadelphia, which was then the capital of our new country. He met Washington at a Christmas party in 1778. Juan fed Washington information obtained from the Spanish government about British troop movements and about Spain and France's counter movements against England. Interesting factoid – Juan's nephew, Pedro 'Peter' Casanave was mayor of Georgetown, Washington, D.C., and directed the construction of the White House actually laying the cornerstone himself in 1792."

Che-Che saw the glaze of indifference that covered Catarina's eyes. She had seen it many, many times before. "Yeah, well, my husband and kids do say that I can clear a room faster than anyone if I get talking about family history and lineage, or Elvis as I do like his music, but that's a story for another day.," she finished.

"Nonsense," Suzanne said, "we love hearing about the Patriots from the Revolutionary War, don't we, Ann?"

"Yes, we do, but I'm sure those without our interest find it just names and dates. That is not how we see it – these are flesh and blood relatives to us," Ann agreed.

"Hmmm, whatever," Catarina said faintly. Che-Che, Suzanne and Ann gave each other a knowing glance. Catarina would not be someone interested enough in family history to include in their genealogical conversations going forward.

Ann looked at her new friend, Che-Che. She was a remarkable woman. A dynamo, a business warrior having started and sold two businesses already. Married young to a lovely but slightly meek man who worked all day and tended his garden in the evenings and weekends when weather permitted. Ann wondered how he filled his free time during the winter months. They had their children, a son and a daughter, early in their marriage, who were now at college and fairly independent. This had freed Che-Che up to devote her non-working time to her passion for family lineage research. When Ann retired from full time police work, she had joined Che-Che and Suzanne in research and interest in the local D.A.R. Chapter. There Ann could involve herself in projects that helped active military personnel, veterans, and the community at large. Che-Che was still working towards Ann's full membership, trying to get all the documentation they needed to link Ann to her most obvious Revolutionary War soldier.

"Che-Che, found anything new for me?" Ann asked as Catarina slowly strayed away, looking at photos on the walls and knick-knacks on the tables and bookcases.

"I'll get back onto that in a bit. I think we are nearly there. I'll just need some photocopies of some things from you," Che-Che answered. Che-Che kept her voice even and her eyes on the keyboard in front of her. She did not want to discuss certain questions she had about Ann and her family, and some information she had found that might be of a sensitive nature in front of Suzanne, the kids or especially this Catarina Blackpaw person. Every nerve in Che-Che's body screamed "BEWARE!" when Catarina came near or spoke. She was going to have to have a discreet conversation with Suzanne about some other things she had discovered on the internet as well. Amazing what one could learn while doing ancestry research.

Chapter 5

July 3

The next morning, Ann and John packed up her books-on-tape and ancient Walkman that Ann assured everyone she did not need to replace with more modern equipment, sunblock and beach chairs and headed down to the water's edge right after a quick cup of coffee. Robin could smell it brewing and hear them moving around, but there was NO WAY she was getting up at 7:00 a.m.. Then her eyes flew open. Wait a minute! In a panic for a brief few seconds, she couldn't remember what time the lifeguards started on duty. She and Caela would want to be there, subtly staked out on their beach blanket near the lifeguard stand.

"Caela, wake up!" Robin slid out of bed and shook Caela until the rubble pile of covers and pillows moved. Robin knew Caela was under there somewhere. "We have to get down to the beach. Get up!"

Once ready and downstairs with the others headed to the beach, Robin asked Caela, "Can you grab that yellow inner tube – it's great fun if it isn't too rough. I want my pink tee-shirt in case the sun gets too hot. I'll run back up and get it and be right back."

Robin lightly scampered back up the staircase and eased in through the door into the living area hallway. She saw Catarina, who was alone and moving through the living room area, lifting up photos and looking at the backs of the frames, turning over lamps and studying their bases, opening drawers and rifling through the contents. Catarina paused when she came to the bottom drawer of the little oak table that stood between two chairs at the far end of the living room.

Catarina was not wearing her eyepatch and she was using both eyes, which were as perfectly normal as Robin's eyes. Robin had stopped dead in her tracks in the doorway watching Catarina in her search of the room, then had eased back out of sight, continuing to peer around the door frame. Catarina pushed the contents from one side to the other, then withdrew the drawer from the table and emptied it out onto the seat of one of the nearby chairs.

Robin knew she was spying, and really should not keep her presence secret out of good manners, but Catarina was acting so bizarrely that Robin forgot herself for those few moments as she just hung back, quietly in the doorway.

Catarina set the little drawer down on top of the things that she had spilled out onto the chair cushion. She reached into her shorts pocket and withdrew her cell phone. After straightening the drawer in the viewfinder, she snapped several photos of the bottom of the empty drawer. Whatever was there on the wood certainly was of interest to her.

Robin knew something odd and very unusual was happening. She stepped silently back through the door, leaving it unlatched so as to not make any noise, and then slowly, carefully went down the staircase to rejoin Caela.

"Where is your tee-shirt?"

"Decided against it. Come on, let's go."

"Okay with me! Let's do this beach and boy thing!" Caela exuberantly agreed.

Robin headed down the sidewalk with Caela, but knew she needed to think about what she had just witnessed. As it turned out, the girls arrived well in advance of the lifeguards. Ann and John had set up near the receding tide line, so Ann could feel the water on her feet, low tide occurring about 10:00 a.m. that morning. There were a couple of joggers headed down the beach, a man with one of those metal detectors weaving his way back and forth across the sand. The girls waved to John as they strategically laid out their beach blanket close to the lifeguard stand such that, when they would be looking up at the lifeguard on duty, anticipating hours of riveting conversation, he wouldn't have to stare into the sun to see them. It would be at least an hour before the lifeguard squad vehicle would come up the beach, dropping each lifeguard and their gear for the day at their chair. Robin sat on the beach blanket, slathered on some SPF8 to get her started in the early morning sun, found some music on her headset and settled in for the wait. She needed to think.

Robin could see her mom had her headset on, too. She had a small cooler at her side – no beer – just Dick Francis mystery books on tape and diet Cokes in there at this early hour. Her mom loved a good mystery and had decided to dedicate the week to her favorite author. Caela was listening to her iPod and reading a required school book she also promised her mom she would finish before returning home. She needed to have it read before the start of the fall school term at the private school she now attended. She knew that if she read early each morning, she'd not only get the book read before returning home, but that she could lay aside the book and her scholarly looking glasses before the hunky lifeguards arrived on the beach. It was the price she had to pay for getting permission from her parents to come along.

Private school had changed the way Caela looked – shorter hair, better clothes, preppy accessories -- but it had not dampened Caela's zest for all the little things in life. Caela could find fun in anything at any time. That's what had drawn Robin to her when they had met the year before at St. Katherine's Church's youth choir rehearsals. They might not see each other during the school day, but they had become fast friends.

Robin got up and went down to where her folks were sitting.

"Tell me what you see," Ann said. Robin would come to know this phrase extremely well over the next few years.

"Well, let's see. Sorry, no pun intended. Catarina is finally headed this way with her beach chair. A few seagulls flying overhead and some standing quietly on the beach. A 'V' pattern of brown pelicans flying down the beach not far over our heads, looking for schools of fish in the shallow water to dive in after. They are weird looking! Sanderlings running down the beach as the waves recede, pecking at the sand for those wormy things and stuff as they go. I like how they try to out-race the waves coming up the beach, like they are afraid to get their feet wet. The old man with the metal detector is coming back up the beach. He stoops down, digs in the sand with a sieve and sees if what the detector has heard is anything good, then he continues on up the beach. If it's no good, he throws it back into the sand. Guess he's looking for money and stuff."

Robin saw the beach patrol Jeep a long way off, excused herself and returned to her stakeout position. She nudged Caela into action. Off came the headset, on went the lip gloss. A lifeguard jumped off the back of the Jeep with his orange buoy and rescue station bag. Robin suspected it was his lunch more than anything else.

"See you later, Roger," he called.

"See you at five, Al."

"Yeah, don't be late!" They laughed and the Jeep drove off. He was medium height and build, dark hair contrary to the myth that all lifeguards are California blondes, and sported a deep tan. He walked past the girls to the elevated wooden chair.

"Hi," Caela ventured, never the shy one, flashing her newly un-braced teeth at him. Robin was jealous, she'd admit it. She had only just received an eighteen-month sentence in her own braces. Ann had told her that she'd be glad to have a beautiful smile for the rest of her life, so just buck up, the time would pass. Robin would have given just about anything for it to have that smile now.

Al looked down at the girls and nodded, then climbed up into the chair. The nod was enough. Enough to cherish all day long, to mull over, to evaluate his every innuendo until tomorrow. Caela and Robin would talk about it until they put out the lights that evening in the bedroom they shared. It would have to do until tomorrow. They recognized that he was the boy from next door to Suzanne's and that the next evening, they would be at his house for the Baby Parade and BBQ, so this was a good way to have introduced themselves in advance of that.

John had bought the local paper at Skipper's, the local beach store, and Robin could hear him reading it out loud to her mom. He loved the local papers wherever he went. Loved the police blotter, the obits, the local stories serving as the de facto social column.

"Another break-in late yesterday afternoon. Just some jewelry taken. You didn't bring anything that you are leaving in the cottage when we're down here, did you?"

"No. I thought we went over this yesterday when I discussed it with the girls. Besides, you know I don't let these rings off my finger! If the guy breaks into Suzanne's cottage, he'll have to settle for dirty towels and sandy sneakers. Actually, my good stuff is in the bank safe deposit box back home. I was afraid the house would get robbed while we were gone. I never dreamed that we'd be in the middle of a string of jewelry heists down here. Maybe I ought to offer to . . ." Ann said to John, thinking of offering to help the local police find the criminals.

Robin wondered why it was that parents always think they know better than anyone else? She cringed at the thought of her half-blind, gimpy mother down at the Ocean City police station voicing her opinions on 'Who Dunnit'. Although, Robin had to admit, her mom had been known to solve more than a few crimes back home.

"No, you don't! You're on vacation, and frankly *out* of that line of work now that you've retired," John said emphatically.

"Semi-Retired, thank you very much," Ann said with a twinkle in her eye and a half-smile.

Al told Caela and Robin about the beach party the lifeguards had the night before. He seemed really talkative; Robin guessed because he'd had such a good time. There had been a bonfire, some music and dancing, the weather had been perfect – quiet receding tide, a light sea breeze, a full moon in a cloudless sky. He told the girls they would really have enjoyed it if they had come along. Yeah, right, like they could have gotten permission to meet lifeguards after dark and party the night away, Robin thought. He didn't know her mom and step-dad! Robin and Caela just nodded in agreement, not willing to let him know that they were so much younger.

"And we even thought we saw the old guy with the metal detector last night. He didn't have his detector with him, he was just slowly walking along, poking at the sand," Al said.

"Guess he just loves the beach," Robin said, her voice sounding unnaturally dry, cracking with the apprehension of actually talking to Al.

"No, just a little kooky, I think. God knows when he sleeps," Al said.

"Quiet, here he comes now," Caela interjected. They turned and saw him parallel to them but down closer to the tideline, sweeping the sand with his metal detector. He turned and looked at Al and the girls, then turned and continued on.

"See, he heard you!" Caela said, mortified they'd been overheard.

"No, I don't think so – not with that headset on," Al replied.

Ann knew Robin and Caela would want their own space on the beach, so she didn't fuss when she saw they were placing their blanket closer to the lifeguard chair than to the spot she and John had staked out for themselves and their friends, who were now slowly making their way down the sand to join them that morning.

Bill and Suzanne chatted away, mostly about nothing, about the beach and what Ocean City had to offer. Suzanne mentioned that some rain was forecast for the day after the 4th July, so they might want to consider a drive down to Cape May to get out of the house, if the weather wasn't going to cooperate for a beach day. Che-Che went into the water for her long swim seemingly oblivious to the water temperature or wave height. Ann admired that Che-Che knew she was capable and wasn't afraid to be active.

When Che-Che returned and had quickly used a towel to get most of the water off her tanned arms and legs and out of her wet hair, she sat with them again. Bill excused himself. He said he'd take a stroll up on the boardwalk to see what's what now that he'd had some time the previous evening to study the Ocean City brochure in his room. John seemed immersed in his newspaper. Che-Che took this opportunity to speak quietly to Suzanne.

"Suzanne, a word?"

"Yes, of course."

"Before Catarina returns, I feel I need to share a couple of things."

Ann was all ears as well. She also had wanted to talk about Catarina, but the opportunity to do so had eluded her. Catarina seemed to know to not leave them alone.

"Don't get me wrong, she seems a – nice – enough person and I know she's family – "

"Well, Frank's family, not really mine – "

"Yes, exactly. My point. What do you know about this stranger sleeping in the hallway outside all our bedrooms?"

"Well, not much. I do know Frank had a cousin named Catarina Blackpaw."

"Any chance she made up that name?"

"No, sadly no. She's the daughter of Frank's mom's sister. Aunt Julia married a man she met up there in Maine as a teenager. His father was Native American. Hence the 'Blackpaw', I guess. I've been trying to remember if she came to our wedding, but it was so long ago – twenty years now, I am drawing a blank. If we were home in Buckelsmere I could pull out the wedding album and take a look at the photos. When Frank died, I started to lose touch with the more distant members of the family. And of course, Frank's folks are dead as well, so I really have had no contact with that side of the family for the last fifteen years."

Che-Che proceeded carefully. "Have you noticed she never initiates a conversation? Never offers any details about her life, her home, her family, anything? After all these years and after having allegedly sought you out here, you'd think she's be talking a blue streak, catching up on all the family news."

"Yes, that is odd, now that you mention it," Suzanne said.

"Che-Che, you've starting to sound like Bill and me – always suspicious of people and their motives," Ann said.

"Well, I think this is just unusual. She shows up uninvited, unexpected. She made sure she is in the house, not lodged at some nearby motel down the beach. She contributes nothing to any conversation we've had for two days now. And -- where is she now? What could she be doing? I for one am uneasy about that. She gives me the creeps."

"She said something about walking along the beach for a while," Suzanne explained.

"Consider this, we don't know *what* she is doing," Che-Che finished. She knew she had spoken her mind, shared as much as she felt she dared share.

Ann decided to continue the conversation. "Suzanne, I'm not saying there is anything amiss, but Che-Che does have a point. What do you know about this woman? She could be an ax-murderer for all we know," Ann paused and then decided to just go ahead and say it, "And yesterday, there was a moment when I was very uncomfortable with her response to her background. I think she did not know that her family was English, Dutch and Italian. Surely, she must have known about the Native American part. I mean, 'Blackpaw'?"

Suzanne stared out from under her large red hat at her friends. "What? What am I to do? Chuck her out, question her? I'm not sure what to do?"

"I think we just need to be aware that at least two of us are not completely sure why she's here. That's all. Maybe we can pull more out of her, get her to confirm she *is* just Frank's cousin dropping in after twenty years to say hello. Let's keep our eyes and ears open. Let's be wary. Let's not be leaving her alone at the house, or especially alone with the girls."

Suzanne pulled her red hat down over her hair more securely, contemplating all that her friends had shared with her. She had only invited Catarina in because who else would present themselves under such odd circumstances. Odd things did happen after all, and Catarina did epitomize the word 'odd', that was for sure.

Che-Che might have been done with the Catarina subject, but now she turned her attention to Ann.

"Ann, a word in *your* ear. I have been working on your family tree in ancestry.com for you. I notice and forgive me for saying so, but you don't have Robin on your tree. I'm wondering about fitting her in. At thirteen, she might be interested in the Children of the American Revolution chapter that meets near us as a prelude to getting her involved at age eighteen as a Junior in the D.A.R."

Ann knew she had to decide. She knew that Suzanne would lower her eyes and say nothing; she'd sit there in the sand until doomsday arrived, but she'd say nothing to Che-Che about this. Suzanne knew most of the story, not all, but she knew enough. But was a loyal and true friend who would keep it all as secret as Ann wished. Ann decided on the short truth. The truth, but not the deep background truth. She had only known Che-Che for about five months, felt like she could trust her, but Robin's safety and well-being came first. Too much information given could never be retracted later. As Ann had predicted, Suzanne had not moved a muscle, perhaps had not even taken a breath, waiting for Ann's answer to Che-Che's seemingly harmless question.

"Robin is adopted. When I was twenty-nine and finishing my Master's Degree in Scotland. She was a foundling, and I took her in. I returned to the States the next summer, settled into police work, married John about five years later and that's really all there is to tell. So, no, Robin's not eligible for C.A.R. and not for D.A.R. through me."

"Oh," Che-Che said in response. "Is she aware?"

"That she's adopted? Yes. Everything else, no, I haven't had any real conversation with her about it. I know it won't be long before she has a terrible longing and urge to know, but frankly, it scares me a bit that when it does happen that I'll lose her, even if it is only a little bit. I've always been her mom. Then one day, she may decide I'm not."

Suzanne reached out and took Ann's hand.

"Never. That will never happen," she assured Ann.

"Well then. I'll downplay the family research talk while we are all together this week. No need to set up any uncomfortable, premature conversations," Che-Che offered.

"Thanks. To both of you. I know I should have initiated that conversation with her already, but with everything that has gone on – my eyes, the broken hip, the move to Buckelsmere – I'm waiting until it all calms down."

Ann was obviously not going to confide anything further, so Che-Che dropped it. Though she did wonder if Ann wasn't perhaps Robin's real mother and who the father would have been. She'd have to decide at a later date if she dared ask Suzanne what more there was to the story, and wondered if Suzanne would tell her if she did know. But seeing Catarina head their way, and sensing that Robin and Caela may have been close enough to hear part of that conversation, if they had been paying attention, Che-Che knew her time had run out.

Robin had indeed heard bits and pieces. She knew that Ann had adopted her as a baby, that John was her stepdad, she remembered the little wedding party that day long ago on a brilliant day in April. Even to her young eyes, it had been special. She really had given no thought to the other true hard facts. She hadn't even decided if she needed to know them. Maybe Che-Che was right – maybe she should ask but what would that change? Would it make things better, or worse, or just different? She didn't know.

Robin saw Catarina approaching, and taking Bill's empty chair. After what she had witnessed that morning back at the house, Robin decided it might be entertaining to go over and listen in. The lifeguards had all shifted down the beach to the next lifeguard chair in rotation, and it was two girl lifeguards who took over Al's chair. She nudged Caela, picked up her towel and moved closer to the adults.

"Sorry, sorry, sorry for my delay. I needed a walk. Lovely day, hot but lovely," Catarina explained quickly.

"Yes, lovely and hot," Che-Che agreed. "Try the water."

"Oh, no. It'd be way too cold for me" Catarina trilled. "No, no, no!"

"I would have thought you'd be used to cold water, being from Maine and all," Ann said, Catarina bristled but kept quiet.

"Oh no! I think I have lost an earring!" Suzanne interrupted, feeling both earlobes.

"It can't be far. Everyone, sift through the sand with your hands," Robin said, starting the process. But after a few minutes, they gave up without finding it.

"Maybe that metal detector guy will find it tonight or tomorrow morning," Suzanne said. "He's always finding one piece of treasure or another."

"Treasure. He finds treasure?" Catarina said, having perked up a bit.

"Well, yes. Jewelry, old English or Spanish coins that wash up from shipwrecks after a storm. But mostly trash and things that people like me just now have lost while on the beach."

"He's actually down the beach, headed this way," Caela said.

"Let me speak to him. Maybe he can find it for you," Catarina said, rising, brushing the sand off her hands and the bottom of her bathing suit. And then she headed down the beach to intercept the metal detectorist. Robin wondered what that was all about? Today's strange developments with Catarina were going to have to be discussed with someone later on, Robin knew.

From his vantage point up on the boardwalk, Bill Dancer looked across the beach towards the ocean. His friends were sitting there together. Sadly, that odd one, Catarina, was sitting in his chair next to Suzanne. If he returned now, he'd not have the advantage of sitting right next to Suzanne.

The Diamond Dunes Murders

Bill had walked on the boardwalk in search of postcards to send home to family, but found none. He must not be looking in the right kind of shops. There were plenty of food vendors and beach paraphernalia stores. But not a one carried post cards.

He treated himself to a grilled pork roll sandwich for Second Breakfast and was surprised how terrific it tasted. It might have ruined other people's appetite for lunch later, but not Bill. Those extra calories would carry him until lunch without a problem. The wood fire gave the pork roll a flavor and crunch that was over-the-top good.

Bill walked down to 9th Street and bought salt water taffy at Shriver's with the coupon in the booklet from his room for his mom, for his three great aunts, and a box to take back to the office for his coworkers at the Buckelsmere Police Station. In business since 1898 the sign said. He watched the taffy machines for a while, twisting and pulling the taffy before it was loaded into the cutting and wrapping machines. He had been amazed at the quantity and range of flavors available. He somehow had been under the impression you 'bought a box of taffy'. This shop had bins and bins of flavors he could mix and match. It had been too difficult to decide. Bill bought a couple of pre-made mixed taffy boxes for the folks back home, and decided on a box mixed between molasses and black walnut that he'd open back at Diamond Dunes that afternoon. He knew Ann loved molasses and Suzanne once had mentioned baking with real black walnuts. They could share that box all week, or until their sweet tooth got the better of them and it was all gone.

He and his sisters would have loved vacationing here as children, but being farm kids, summer vacations meant doing chores around the farm when the extra sets of hands were more than welcome. Bill knew he loved the beach after only these two days. This beach. Suzanne's beach. He thought of her and the old house she called Diamond Dunes that she had inherited. He hoped she'd keep it forever and not forget to invite him again.

Shelly Young Bell

Bill watched Catarina rise from his beach chair and walk south along the beach until she met up with the man using the metal detector. Catarina talked with him, getting progressively closer as she talked, implying what exactly, intimacy? Sharing a secret? Making plans? Bill made a mental note to ask Ann about it later. He did not like this dark, petite, eye-patched, upstart that had gate crashed their happy holiday. He did not care for her one tiny bit.

The Diamond Dunes Murders

Dear Aunt Helen, Aunt Dot and Aunt Jan,

Didn't know I'd enjoy this beach vacation as much as I am. Good friends, good food, *great* weather so far. And even better news to share – I heard that my novel has been accepted for publication in the fall! I should have it in time for the Writer's Conference in November.

Your loving grand-nephew,
Bill

Chapter 6

Cocktail Hour, July 3

While Suzanne, Ann and the girls kept busy in the kitchen preparing things for the rooftop deck cocktail and dancing party planned for later that afternoon, Bill and John excused themselves to the back porch off the living area to stay out from under the ladies' feet. In the shade, screened in against the flies, and with a cooling breeze wafting through the floor to ceiling screened walls, they relaxed on the antique wicker chairs, content and tired after their hours of beach time that morning and their satisfying lunch.

"So, Bill, what do you make of this Catarina character," John asked quietly, not quite sure where said character currently was.

Bill, as well, glanced around before answering quietly. "Strange bird. Strange looking. Strange acting. Not friendly really – which you'd think a party crasher would try to be. Anti-social. I mean, where is she right now, I wonder? Not laying on her cot in the hallway, for sure. I have to admit, I kept my bedroom door bolted last night, as I advised Robin and Caela to do as well. Don't tell Ann, I don't want her thinking I know something, which I don't."

John thought about this before answering. "I am wondering several things, now that it is day two of our beach week and apparently this Catarina is determined to stay. One – why? Why is this cousin of Suzanne's late husband so interested in spending time with people she doesn't know and isn't trying to get to know? Two – she has shared nothing with us; she has asked a fair number of questions of us, but we have learned nothing further about her since her initial 'I am Frank's cousin' story on day one. Three – do you think, as the police detective that you are, that you and I ought to do something about finding out about her? I mean, she could be an escaped lunatic for all we know!"

Bill smiled. "We'll make a detective out of you yet, John. You are asking some of the same questions I've been asking myself. I'd like to press Suzanne about it, but I don't want to dredge up the past, of any unhappy memories of Frank's passing and all. But I don't think Suzanne is being assertive enough to find out why this Catarina is here."

"Yes, I get that. I know that you have an interest in keeping your interactions with Suzanne positive. Don't look so surprised, everyone can see it on both of your faces so I suggest you just get on with it. I think I understand your feelings. I remember back with I first met Ann. I was being careful with her; trying so hard to become part of her life. I was afraid I'd overstep, or not step far enough soon enough. I tried to just be myself, but I was so desperately in love with her that I was equally as desperate not to screw up my chances with her. As today's kids would say, I was a hot mess!" John paused. "Sorry, I don't mean to project all that on how you are feeling, and onto your friendship with Suzanne."

"No, John, that's okay. I am careful, I admit. I am being way too cautious, I think, but like you, what if I overstep, say something that drives her to not want to see me again. I don't know how I'd bear that," Bill confessed.

"Sorry, I have no really good advice when it comes to women. But Suzanne is a lovely, level-headed woman. I can see in her eyes that it is more than casual affection that she has for you. Just keep going. Though keep in mind – time, biological clocks, you know."

"Yes, I do. I think I could be persuaded either way she decided, children or no children. But I do know if I don't move this along, she might lose what is already a small window of opportunity."

"Back to Catarina. What do you think, Bill?"

"I think we ought to be careful. I think I ought to do a background check. It will only take a phone call. The boys at the office will be glad for something a bit out of the ordinary to do. I won't go into too much detail with them, don't worry. I think it will either show us that there is nothing to worry about and we should just endure her for a few days, or will prove we have a great deal to be concerned about and then we can decide the best action to take. I think we need more information, more hard facts from outside sources first. In the meantime, we will continue to wait and watch, and be thinking about how to handle it if we have to get her out of here."

John was about to agree when the door squeaked as it opened and Robin came out to join them. John and Bill looked at each to acknowledge her presence and that their conversation was at an end for the time being. As if reading each other's thoughts, John and Bill each gave the other the briefest of nods.

"What you two doing out here?" Robin asked.

"Nothing. Just talking," John said.

"I bet you were talking about our Miss Catarina Blackpaw," Robin said. Bill and John tried hard not to react – how did girls always know these things? Were they all psychic? Robin saw the rigid reaction her question got and knew she had been correct.

"Can I share something? Something that happened earlier, and I haven't told anyone?" Robin asked in such a serious and sotto voce that Bill and John weren't sure they had actually heard her say it.

Robin continued, "I didn't really come out here to say this. But I think I will since I have the two of you here alone. I don't want to keep it to myself any longer. It's beginning to upset me."

John reached out and took her hand, drawing Robin down into the chair next to him. "It's okay. Don't be upset. What is the problem, exactly?" he asked her.

Robin looked up at John's face and then at Bill who had that 'I don't know how to handle upset women' look that he got whenever he was confronted with any moments of her teenage angst. Not that she was given to tears often, but she knew Bill just didn't have a lot of experience with it. It gave her an odd sense of comfort that John was always patient and that Bill was always a bit afraid. They were so themselves, all the time.

"Promise. Promise me that this stays between the three of us. Please promise you won't go charging in there screaming and yelling. Promise?"

John spoke first. "Robin, if it will relieve your fear over telling this secret, then yes, I promise no screaming, yelling or even telling. And I am sure Bill feels the same way. We will sit here quietly, absorb what you tell us and not overreact. That's really what you want, right, just that we don't overreact?" John asked, trying to keep Robin calm. Yet inside himself, John was becoming increasingly agitated, and a bit afraid what was so upsetting that Robin had phrased it all as she had.

"Okay," Robin said, pausing, then after a deep breath she continued. "That Catarina is a liar. Yes, a liar, let me finish before you start. She is lying about the eyepatch. I saw her take it off earlier today. And she then was searching the house for something. I don't know what. It was first thing this morning, when everyone else was downstairs just starting out for the beach. I had forgotten my pink beach shirt. I decided to come back upstairs to get it, and that's when I found her – eyepatch off, flipped up onto her forehead, going through the living area, opening everything, turning everything upside own, searching everywhere," Robin paused to raise her hand to stop the two men from beginning to speak or ask questions, "I know if you confront her she will just say I made the whole thing up, and I am afraid what she might do to me, what stories she might make up about me to get back at me for telling on her. I don't want to be a rat, that's the correct word, rat, right? But I figure if she is lying about the eyepatch, and was searching Suzanne's things, what else might she do or already have done? I should tell you, right?" Robin asked, needing their confirmation.

"Yes, yes of course, dear, you should have told us, and we are so very glad you did. Bill and I have had our doubts and suspicions as well. It might be better not to discuss this with anyone else just yet, until Bill and

I can figure out what is going on. Don't repeat any of this to Caela. Hopefully you haven't already; and leave it to me and Bill to discuss with your mom and Suzanne. And if you notice anything else odd let Bill or me know. We will take care of things," John assured her.

Robin nodded in agreement. Bill and John looked at each other, well aware that there was probably no time to lose in putting their plans into action.

"I think it might be a good idea if you and Caela ran up to the store for me. Get out of the house for a little bit. You can clear your head, take your mind off all this, consider it now in our hands and you can just go back to having a good time. What do you say? Bill and I will start the process of getting Catarina to leave, although it might take a day or two, *if* you were serious about the no screaming and yelling and telling part!" John finished with a smile.

"Oh, John!" Robin said, smiling herself. Bill pulled a $10.00 dollar bill out of his wallet and gave it to Robin. "Get a couple more newspapers for John, and I need three postage stamps. See if you and Caela can locate them for me, and you can spend the rest of the ten dollars on whatever you'd like."

"Gee, thanks, Bill!" Robin said fingering the $10.00 before sticking it into her shorts pocket, and scampering off to find Caela for their errand.

"I'd say I was shocked, but somehow I am not," John said.

"I know. The situation has now taken some turns we weren't expecting. I knew something was up, but searching Suzanne's house – what does she expect to find? Anyone can see, there is nothing here of value, in case it is all lost to a hurricane. Time for me to excuse myself to my room, I have a phone call to make. It might take until tomorrow or the next day until I get any real information back. Meanwhile, keep your eyes on the girls to be sure they are out of Catarina's grasp. I think the rest of us could handle ourselves against her if it came to that. I need to talk with Suzanne about the Catarina this woman is supposed to be. After all, she very well might be the Catarina Blackpaw from Maine, Frank's long-lost cousin, just here for a long overdue visit. But the detective in me says not." Bill rose and headed inside where he would try to get Suzanne alone for a few minutes for that pointed conversation.

Bill found her coming down from the bedroom level, having changed into a peach colored sundress for their rooftop soiree later. It showed off her tan, and her lovely figure. Bill tried hard to focus on the matter at hand. He led her down the hallway towards Ann and John's bedroom at the front of the house, out of anyone's range of hearing.

"Where's Catarina?" Bill asked

"In the bathroom, I think," Suzanne answered. "It's the only place she can get any privacy, she said."

"Tell me more about her, anything, everything," Bill said.

"Why, What's wrong? What's happened?" Suzanne asked in rising alarm.

"Nothing, nothing. Just curious. Trying to piece some things together," Bill soothed.

"No, it's something. I've sensed it in everyone since her arrival. I only know she is Frank's first cousin. They saw each other summers when they were kids. I keep thinking she will tell us what prompted her to get in touch now, why she drove ten hours to see me here at Diamond Dunes when she hasn't called, sent a Christmas Card – nothing for more than fifteen years. I mean, it could happen right? She could just be wanting to pick up the family relationship that she let lapse?

"Oh sure, I suppose. It would be a help if you would do a couple of things, get Ann and Che-Che to help as well. It will look more natural if the group is having a conversation about things, I will watch and analyze her reactions and comments. Maybe she won't like it and decide she's had enough family beach time and go home. That would be best. I understand you don't want a scene, none of us do, so here's what I would like you to do," Bill said, and then explained what he would like her to introduce into the conversation.

They were sitting around the dining room table when Catarina finally joined them that afternoon. Che-Che was talking about ancestors, as she so often did. Catarina decided to pour herself an iced tea first, then sat at the kitchen island while she listened in.

"Suzanne, I see here on Frank's family tree that way back, he had an Italian ancestor, Constanti Spinelli, that moved from northern Italy near Milan to Antwerp, Belgium area in the 1500's. And that her father, Tommaso di Guasparre Spinelli was Italian obviously as well. Her mother, *Catarina* de Cordes was born in Antwerp. Cordes sounds Spanish; that might be interesting for me to explore! I will let you know what I find out. Isn't that interesting? Another Catarina in the family way back that far? Catarina, maybe you were named after her? This Catarina was the mother of that ancestral line's first immigrant to America," Che-Che casually asked her. The color rose up Catarina's neck and onto her face. Bill watched the reaction carefully. Catarina had no way of knowing if what Che-Che was saying was true, or if Che-Che was actually reading these things off the computer screen in front of her, or if perhaps they were joking her. Bill watched for anything that would give him a clue about what Catarina might be thinking – a movement, breathing patterns, facial coloring.

Che-Che continued, "My, my. This Catarina's uncle was the Canon at the Florence Cathedral. Someone in a high place of power. Interesting. Florence, the Medici's, the Florentine diamond. I see something happening there. Antwerp was the site of eighty-five percent of the world's diamond trade at that time. This Catarina's father travelled back and forth between Antwerp and Florence according to the records here in this Wikipedia article. He must have been in the diamond trade. This diamond, the Florentine Diamond, ended up in the hands of the Medici's. What do you think about that?"

Catarina nearly spilled her drink when Che-Che mentioned the Florentine Diamond. Not unnoticed by Bill, John and Suzanne. Suzanne played dumb. "Gee, Catarina, that would be something wouldn't it?

Diamonds and dukes, treasure and travel – all in Frank and your family's background."

"I, I, yes, of course. Of course, if you say so. I don't really know anything about that . . ."

"Well, Che-Che, when we get home to Bucklesmere, we'll have to check it out more thoroughly," Suzanne said.

"Home? Buckelsmere? I thought this was your home?" Catarina asked, stuttering and letting her guard down just for that brief comment.

"Oh, no, this is only a summer place really. I live in the Beck family home in Buckelsmere, Pennsylvania. I only come here for the summers," Suzanne clarified, rather surprised that Catarina did not remember that the family had always lived in Bucks County, Pennsylvania, especially since she had probably attended Suzanne and Frank's wedding at St. Katherine's in Buckelsmere.

"Frank's father's house?" Catarina's voice had a twinge of alarm, not unnoticed by Bill.

"Yes," Suzanne answered.

"You mean, there's more of Uncle Aldo's things that are not here, at this house," Catarina asked.

"Well, yes. I left the old beachy furniture that was here. I covered all the seat cushions with updated fabric, spray painted all the wicker – you know, freshening it up a century or two!" Suzanne shared, waving her hand towards the living room seating area, trying to keep the mood light and not give away her apprehension.

"And lovely it is," agreed Che-Che.

Ann listened to all of this and wondered. She turned and watched Bill closely. Where was this conversation going? And why had Bill sent the girls on his mid-afternoon errand in the heat. Ann could feel the tension and could sense that way more was going on here this afternoon than a casual conversation about ancient Italian history and family lines. She saw that Bill had his work face on. And John was watching Catarina with a sharpness usually reserved for the Sunday New York Time's crossword puzzle or for when he was preparing their taxes. Ann had not been prewarned that they were going to stage something and wondered why not? But she'd sit tight, watch and wait, it would become clear eventually.

Catarina's mind was whirling, but she was still unaware she was being manipulated and that several of them were leading her ever so close to the brink of disclosure.

"Nothing of value here, can't be really. One gets a few days' notice of a hurricane making a direct hit, but that would not be enough time to get here from home, board up the house, and move a houseful of things to safety all by myself. I have to consider everything here as disposable. I was lucky that when the last major hurricane hit it was farther north. No real damage happened here. And luckily Aldo had the foresight to build this house on pilings so it is saved from the most casual of flooding.

"Which reminds me, they are calling for street flooding a couple of nights from now. One of those perfect full moon-high tide-storm front situations that happen a few times a year. We will want to be sure to bring anything important up off street level, perhaps even move the cars to a parking lot up the block at the Catholic church which must be a foot or two higher than here as it never floods there."

Bill knew he had to stop the conversation before it got to the point of accusation and denial. He did not want to tip their hand quite yet and let Catarina know that they suspected she was a fraud.

"When the girls get back, I hope it will be time for cocktails and dancing," Bill said, smiling at them all, changing the subject from the Beck family's Italian roots, Medici treasure and the house in Buckelsmere. "I am very much looking forward to the crab dip you made and some cold prosecco. It's nice it has cooled off a bit. Better for dancing. Perhaps we'll have a glorious sunset," he said smiling at the others, signaling that the game was hereby suspended for the time being.

Suzanne smiled back at him, "Oh yes, the dip's mixed and mellowing in the refrigerator as we speak. I am thinking that at about 4:00 p.m. we'll take everything upstairs to the roof deck." She checked her watch. "Gee, almost time already. Where did the afternoon go?"

Che-Che gave a couple of quiet cluck-cluck's and powered-down her laptop, knowing what she had learned would provide fodder for later conversation. Che-Che did wonder if it was as obvious to Suzanne and to that wonderfully hunky detective Bill Dancer that this Catarina didn't know her family history (but so many people didn't, it was true!) nor that Suzanne called Buckelsmere home, not here. So very odd.

Chapter 7

Evening, July 3

As Suzanne pulled the appetizers out of the refrigerator, she took the plastic wrap and lids off trays and bowls, placing serving spoons and tongs in everything. She lined it all up on the island, along with opened bottles of wine, and the sparkling Prosecco Bill had brought. It all had to be carried up the two flights of stairs to the roof top deck. Suzanne planned to have cocktails and dancing before they indulged in the BBQ chicken and mixed grilled potatoes and vegetables that she had previously prepared and chilled. She would slide the supper into the warm oven on a very low setting so it would all be heated through before they wanted it later on. Then they would enjoy fruit kabobs and sherbet as they sat around waiting for the sunset. Suzanne suspected no one would be too hungry after the abundant and extravagant appetizers -- cold shrimp and sauces, crab dip, what was left of Bill's pineapple cheese ball and veggies, potato chips, little smoked hot dogs in a BBQ sauce -- so she had kept the main course of supper simple and light.

The roof deck sprawled the width and depth of the house, with a railing all the way around to prevent stepping off into four stories of air. Built-in seating wrapped around three sides; the fourth side sported a waist high counter over cabinets that allowed for storage with a large worktop. Suzanne spent so much time here at Diamond Dunes alone that she had let all the supplies up here run down to just some cans of Coke and a few paper cups. Any ice she needed for tonight she had brought up earlier and stashed in the counter top ice bucket when she and Che-Che had brought up the other paper goods, plasticware, more soda and a radio/CD player with an extension cord. Suzanne was determined to have dancing and you couldn't have dancing without music, after all. Che-Che had been none too complimentary about the selection of music upon which Suzanne had decided.

Caela and Robin had plucked up enough courage to ask Suzanne if they might invite Al from next door to join them, as they then would have someone with whom to dance. Suzanne had readily agreed, as it seemed the best way to have the two teens enjoy themselves at what would otherwise appear as old fogey's party. Al had appeared shortly after his lifeguard shift ended, his dark hair still wet from the shower, just in time to help carry things when Suzanne started handing food and drink items out, directing the party to move upstairs. If everyone carried something, it would all get done in just one trip. The food was to be arranged on the counter top of the cabinet.

"Thanks for asking me. It was going to be deadly at home tonight. Kathy's in-laws are here. Too many people underfoot, no one interesting for me to talk to, and little Jack seems to think that all his toys ought to be strewn all over the floor at all times!! That proves very dangerous if you walk around barefoot!" Al said to them.

"I thought you liked Jack." Suzanne observed.

"I do, but you know – first baby, first grandchild – and way too much stuff! And I have absolutely nothing to talk to Kathy's in-laws about. I might as well be invisible."

"Well, now, it's just that they are all older and have lived in a different era. When you think about it, they are old enough to be your *grandparents*. Kathy is twelve years older than you, and her husband is another six years older than Kathy – so Stephen's parents are twenty years older than might have been the case. Even though socially they are only one generation away from you, they are a lot older than that might indicate.

"You are more than welcome to hang out here tonight. We'll be over at your house tomorrow night for the Baby Parade and the BBQ that your folks are giving. I am so looking forward to your mom's ribs – melt in your mouth tender!" Suzanne assured him.

Caela came and drew Al away. The three younger ones went to the stack of CD's and had some good laughs as they tried to pick from the Frank Sinatra, big bands, Jackie Gleason and generic Dance Party albums. Al snuck a couple of his own CDs into the pile to liven things up a bit later.

"Let me," Robin said, "I know just a little about Frank Sinatra – 'Mr. S' as we call him at home, Here put this one on first," she said handing a CD over to Caela who popped it into the CD player.

While they all listened to Frank croon the first few songs and tried to work their courage up to dance, they ate shrimp and taquitos, chips and crab dip, and the leftover pineapple pepper cheese ball.

Catarina seemed to be trying to be overly friendly to all of them since this afternoon's revelations. Chatty over nothing. She made the rounds trying to strike up a conversation with anyone that would. The change from the standoffish Catarina to social butterfly Catarina was too obvious to ignore. Whatever agenda in which she was now engaged was not being received well by the others. She tried being clingy to Bill, talking to him, batting her one set of eyelashes at him a bit, playing up to his male nature. Bill was having none of it, even finding it a bit annoying. No matter how much she tried to get on an even keel with him, he just tried to fend her off.

Suzanne noticed Catarina trying to monopolize Bill's conversation and attention, but what was she to do? She had no claim on him. At the point Catarina laid her hand on Bill's arm, Suzanne had to turn away, so she did not have to watch. She had to admit to herself that her feelings towards Bill were growing stronger and she found herself thinking about him in ways that a casual friend would definitely not! It didn't help that Che-Che kept referring to his attractiveness.

"So, Bill you're a cop?" Catarina asked.

"Yes, I have always been 'a cop'," Bill said keeping his answer short.

"Must be exciting."

"No, not always. Often it's just paperwork."

"Hmm. Tell me about your most heroic deed," Catarina said.

"Saved a dog from a pond once," Bill said, not pleased he was having to talk about work, about himself, with this woman he was supposed to be watching, not the other way around. Bill watched as John took Ann's hand and encouraged her up off her seat and out to the center of the roof deck, where he gathered her up into his arms and danced, cheek to cheek just as the music admonished. John smiled and whispered over the music into Ann's ear which made her laugh – a happy laugh about something shared by just the two of them. Bill watched as Al took Caela's hand and started his best but awkward attempt of dancing with her; Caela, not caring how poorly they looked, loved every second of it. Catarina's body language radiated her expectations of being asked to dance; Bill could feel them without even having to look at her. Bill was *not* going to ask Catarina to dance, regardless of how close she was standing to him. He was not!

Robin walked across to where he was standing, ignoring Catarina's chit-chat in his ear.

"Bill," Robin addressed him.

"Yes?" Bill answered and gladly took a step away from Catarina.

"You're up," Robin instructed him, motioning with her head towards Suzanne, who stood at the cabinet, refilling her drink, resolutely ignoring what she feared might be going on between Bill and Catarina. Bill looked from Robin with her young face and pure thoughts to Suzanne with her womanly knowledge and passions, then back to Robin. Maybe he should just dance with Robin and be done with it, he was thinking.

Robin shook her head with a smile, and gave his arm a very gentle push towards Suzanne. "No, go. Dance with her. Now."

Bill smiled at Robin, gave Catarina a curt, "Excuse me," and walked over to where Suzanne stood. He took her in his arms, not taking no for an answer, and swept her out, dancing as lightly as a professional. By way of explanation to Suzanne, he said "I learned to dance as a kid, the benefit of having older sisters and girl cousins. It has come in mighty handy with the ladies since then, I might add. I am a most sought after 'plus one' for a wedding." Bill smiled at her, and held Suzanne as close as he could, as close as he had thought about doing night after night. The music and the dancing were his opportunity.

The music changed to 'The Way You Look Tonight.' Bill looked deep into Suzanne's coffee colored eyes. It was where he had first met her, over a cup of coffee. He was suddenly filled with a burst of happiness. Someday, I'll dance to this song at my wedding, he thought to himself as they clung to each other as if they were a well-rehearsed team.

Catarina, miffed at her exclusion, perturbed by the glitch in trying to soften Bill towards her, strutted off to sit by herself in a corner, nursing a glass of white wine and sucking on a celery stick, overlooking the street below.

Robin went to the opposite side and sat with Che-Che, their backs to the sun, which was starting its descent towards a showy orange, red and purple sunset.

Che-Che cluck-clucked at Robin with a smile, "I saw what you did there."

"Couldn't be helped. He needed to be away from that Catarina, and he needed to dance with Suzanne. Period. So, I fixed it," Robin explained.

"Yes, I can see that. You fixed it," Che-Che said with humor in her voice and eyes. They sat a while in silence enjoying the breeze, the music, the dancing.

"Can I ask you something, Che-Che, girl to girl?"

"Sure, honey, anything."

Robin hesitated, watching her mom and step-dad enjoy the music and dancing together – together and apart from everyone else. She watched Bill dance with Suzanne – something totally different there – almost like a secret being told – something so new yet familiar. And of course, Caela and Al, which was just comical, nothing there but teenage attraction. Robin wondered about Che-Che.

"You aren't dancing. Is that because your husband is not here?" Robin asked.

"No, not at all. I'd dance with anyone. Hopefully one of those men will get around to asking me to dance. I do a mean tango! Does it bother you that *you* don't have a partner?" Che-Che asked.

"What do you mean? That I'm not dancing?"

"No, that you, like me, don't have someone here for this party. Someone special. Your mom's husband is here, I suspect Suzanne's next husband is here, forget about that Al character! Is that bothering you?"

"No, I don't think so. I'm only thirteen!"

"Thirteen maybe, but with the heart and sensitivity of one much older. I can see that. If you're feeling a little left out, don't. There will be a time and place where you will be dancing with some wonderful man. Don't worry, and don't be in a rush."

"You sound so wise, Che-Che."

"Heck no, just have done a lot of living, made my fair share of mistakes, borne the bruises, when necessary, celebrated when times were good."

"But not everything turns out okay, does it? Not like in the movies."

"No, of course not, not everyone wins, not everyone survives. Things are never neat."

"I heard my mom tell you I'm adopted. That I will not be able to be in C.A.R. nor D.A.R."

"Don't let that worry you. We enjoy it for the family history it promotes and for the charity works we get to do. But everyone should find their *own* niche, their *own* place of happiness and comfort. I know you sing. I suspect you will find places and groups and events that will mean a great deal more to you than a bunch of old ladies looking at a list of dead relatives. Family history research is my passion, yes, but it does not need to be anyone else's. My kids hate it! True story! Hate it when I bring it up. But they are happy in what they have chosen for themselves. And you know what, I am totally okay with that. Maybe you'd like to meet them sometime. They are older, college aged, but I think you'd like them. Don't worry. Your mom, Ann, she will be okay with what you choose and where you go in life. Just go forward with courage and faith. It will all work out. I see high things for you – always remember that. Don't settle for less than that. It will all be okay, you'll see."

"Everyone seems to have someone. I am not sure I even belong here anymore."

"You belong. Don't you ever worry about that."

And with that, the music ended.

Che-Che called out, "Enough of this tame stuff. Next time I'm picking the playlist. We need something with a Latin beat now!

Chapter 8

July 4th

The 4th of July could not have dawned brighter and bluer. It was going to be a hot one as the sun climbed up through the totally clear sky. No haze, not even a single puffy summer cloud. The air was almost liquid it was so pure; almost as if you could touch the dome of blue overhead. The breeze off the ocean was cool enough that their morning on the beach would be tolerable.

But Catarina had other plans. As the house guests packed up their beach gear and headed out to walk to the beach, she begged off, claiming she had a headache and would sit in a dark room until it passed. She assured them all that they should all go and have a good time, as yes it did seem like it would be a legendary July 4th on the beach, a day designed by the beach angels, and not to worry about her. Two Advil tablets and a couple hours – that's all she needed to be right as rain for the parade and BBQ later.

Bill and John looked at each other, but they both knew that there was nothing in the house worth stealing. She'd already had enough time alone there if she was determined to go through any wallets or purses to steal personal information. They each wanted to comment to the other, but refrained. The look that passed between them was clearly a 'wait until we're down the sidewalk' sort of look. They both clearly knew what the other man was thinking.

Once they all had descended the staircase, Catarina closed the door on the landing firmly. She flipped off the eyepatch and went out to stand on the balcony off her little sleeping alcove that faced the street. She quickly dialed her new friend, the beach detectorist, Carl, on her cell phone when she lost sight of Suzanne and her friends walking towards the beach.

"Hello?" a man answered.

"All clear. How soon can you be here?" Catarina asked.

"Give me five minutes, then my metal detector will be at full power," he answered.

"Okay, but waste no time. We need every second that we can get," Catarina admonished him, and hung up. She checked the time on the cell phone, knowing it would more realistically be ten or fifteen minutes before he turned up. She headed towards the staircase and descended to the ground level parking area and checked her phone again. Maybe another five minutes. She hoped Carl would be swift, yet unnoticed by anyone else when he did arrive.

Catarina spotted him when he was still half a block away, walking swifter than she feared he might; not hurrying, but moving along at a fair clip. He turned into the driveway and in a few strides was underneath the house. They did not speak, but moved directly to the staircase and went up to the living area level.

"No, let's start at the very top and work down," Carl said, looking around.

"Okay, roof deck two stories up," Catarina advised and up they went.

"Don't expect much from this," Carl advised her. "We will probably see a lot of nails and metal electrical boxes, but they will be where we expect they should be. We're looking for readings where there should be none."

When they reached the roof deck, he looked around, put his earphones on, flipped the switch and adjusted a dial. "Stand back and stay quiet," he said to Catarina. Carl swept up and down the deck, swept the head of the detector along the top and sides of the cabinet – nothing.

"Okay, let's head down," Carl said and as they descended the staircase, Carl left the machine on checking the staircase as well as the ceiling areas and every step. Nothing.

On the bedroom level, Carl started at the front of the house, pointing at the cot in the hallway, and looking at Catarina, "Gee, that's all the 'Cousin' is given as accommodations?" and Carl laughed a dry throaty cigarette smoker's laugh.

"Get back to work," Catarina said, "I'm worried now – yesterday she said this is not the only house she has. I was misled when I researched property owned by 'cousin' Frank Beck."

"You said she had treasure hidden here. Are you now telling me there isn't?"

"There might be, that's why you're here checking. I've searched the best I can – in every piece of furniture, I have felt every pillow, I've taken every picture off the wall, I've stepped on every floorboard looking for a loose one, I've done everything you suggested short of taking the walls down."

"Let's see what we find," Carl said patting his metal detector. "But there had better be something – you promised me half of what we find!"

"Just get on with it," Catarina directed. Carl scanned all the walls, the ceilings, the floors. Other than it detecting where there were known electrical and plumbing, nothing else set off the detector. When they reached the living area, Catarina showed him the odd symbols that she had found previously in the drawer of the small table.

"That's crazy. Doesn't make sense to me," Carl said.

"I think it is some kind of code. After all, my father and Suzanne's father-in-law were in the army together, and used code all the time so the Nazis couldn't figure out what they were saying."

"Still, it makes no sense. We're here in New Jersey, not in Nazi Europe."

"No. Well, I just hoped it was something."

"Did you look under each drawer – sometimes things get taped to the bottom of drawers," Carl wanted to know.

"Yes, everywhere you suggested. Besides, if the story my father told me is true, and I have no doubt that it is true, Suzanne's father-in-law's half of the fortune was too large to be taped to the bottom of a drawer."

Carl persisted, checking everything he could, but with no luck.

"Not here. You know she could have moved it to a safe deposit box or someplace else. Maybe if we talked with her, gave her a reason to let us know where it is," Carl suggested. Catarina's initial response was negative, but upon reflection, maybe a little chat, a small bit of pressure might persuade Miss Perfect Suzanne Beck to share the whereabouts of Aldo's treasure. Catarina did not want to believe that Frank and his dad had cashed in all those jewels and spent it all, even though she was well aware that her father had burnt through his half of the treasure fairly easily and quickly.

"Careful there, you're dumping sand out of that thing all over!" Catarina cautioned him, then returned to their conversation about pressuring Suzanne. "Remember Suzanne wears that big red sun hat on the beach. Maybe tomorrow you could talk with her. I'll let you know. Let me think about this. I'll be in touch."

Carl smiled to himself as Catarina let him out at the ground level parking area. He'd talk to Suzanne all right, and if she did tell him where the treasure was, here or anywhere else, it would be his. None of this splitting it 50-50 with this ridiculous Catarina imposter. He'd get the treasure and leave town. Carl thought about what that would entail. He would have been moving on at the end of the summer anyway. He'd have to ditch his current pay-as-you-go cell phone. He'd pack his truck with his equipment and head somewhere better, somewhere he was not known. He smiled, making premature plans to trade in the truck for a new one.

Once he was gone, Catarina walked back through the house, making sure doors and drawers were as they had been left by the other house guests. No need stirring up suspicions. She had to admit to herself she was very disappointed that Carl's search with his equipment had turned up nothing.

Her father had told her many times about how he and Aldo had come upon the chance to return from war-torn Europe with a sack of jewels. Her father had long ago sold his and spent the proceeds. She suspected he must have gambled a good share of it away, or invested it in poor and unproductive schemes, as it was gone before she had reached adulthood. He had gone to his grave still jawing about how he wished he could get hold of Aldo's half. She had known enough of the story to piece together who might now be in possession of it – Suzanne Beck, Frank's widow. Frank was Aldo's only child. The internet had helped with some of the facts, but apparently not enough. Suzanne had mentioned another house in Pennsylvania. Catarina could keep up this ruse a long time if she had to. She'd be out of here as soon as the others left, and she'd somehow follow them back to Suzanne's other house. After all, she was now being the best houseguest and 'cousin' one could imagine. Catarina smiled broadly. 'Gosh, and my headache vanished so quickly in the quiet,' she practiced saying. She glanced at her phone. The group would be back from the beach soon for lunch, then the BBQ and Baby Parade next door with those horrid people. But she'd suck it up and play along to do her best to get information out of Suzanne tonight before she decided if Carl should be encouraged to coax it out of Suzanne. That would be crossing a line she was not sure she wanted to cross just yet.

Chapter 9

Evening, July 4th

Al, for some opportune reason, had July 4th off from his lifeguarding duties starting mid-afternoon, so he wandered over to Suzanne's under the pretense of helping Suzanne carry any food items and chairs across to his folks' house for the neighborhood Baby Parade and BBQ that would follow.

Both Robin and Caela were in the outside showers, giggling through the wood slats to each other over being naked yet so close to a lifeguard passing by them. If Al was aware that they were in the showers, he did not let them know it. He skipped through the propped open door and up the staircase calling out to Suzanne as he went.

"Suzanne, I'm here for carrying duty! Actually, I am here for sanity and a cold drink before the nonsense starts at my house."

Suzanne was pouring freshly made Arnold Palmers into tall glasses, so she handed one over to him. Al swallowed it down in a few gulps and held it out for a refill. Suzanne smiled, knowing he'd spent his work day in the sun and the heat of this perfect July day. "Here, have another," she said and watched him down the second glass as fast as the first. "The girls will be up in a few minutes. I think they are still showering," Suzanne said, watching for his reaction. She thought he looked startled when he realized he had walked right past two teenage girls taking showers without knowing it.

"Okay, I'll wait. Be glad to wait. Way too many people at my house."

"And our added number will only make it worse," Suanne suggested, not believing that Michael and Wendy would think it too many. Always the generous hosts, the Willis' July 4th BBQ was legendary, and acquiring an invitation was always considered a real coup among the neighbors.

"Well, Kathy, Stephen and baby Jack are here at the shore house, and Stephen's parents arrived two days ago. I think you've met them. Later today, mom's sister and my cousin and her girls will be coming over. Everyone wants to see Jack in the Baby Parade."

"Seems like yesterday that you, and Kathy before you, were being pushed around the street out front in the Parade," Suzanne said.

"Yeah, I still remember it, first being pulled around in a wagon, and then eventually being old enough to decorate my bike and ride it around with the older kids. That was the best!"

Suzanne explained to Ann and the others that were sitting nearby at the island and in the dining room area, "Access to our two-block street closes at 6:00 p.m.. A couple of the dads stand guard at the end up by the main north-south street, turning away all cars. Then the bikes and wagons and baby carriages do a two-lap circuit. Everyone decorates their 'ride' with all sorts of red, white and blue decorations and flags. It's a lovely and fun tradition. The kids are so excited. We always have a huge turnout. Some years, I think that kids from surrounding streets must join in as well. There are no prizes or anything, but it really is the highlight of the holiday for the neighborhood. Little Jack will have a large audience if what you are saying is true."

"I think my mom mentioned twenty for BBQ," Al said.

"I have a tray of veggies and dip to take over in advance of the parade. Then I have the pans of baked beans and potato salad to help with dinner. I can't wait for your mom's BBQ ribs. They are so good. I probably have said that before," Suzanne admitted to the good-natured smiles of her friends.

Robin and Caela arrived at that point, washed and dressed. The air-conditioned living space felt so good after the full sun of the beach. They had spent extra time on the beach today, staying after the others had returned home at lunchtime. Sunbathing, playing in the waves with Suzanne's oversized yellow inner tube, and talking with Al and Roger when possible.

Catarina rose from her seat in the living room and came forward toward the kitchen work area. "Anything I can do?" she asked, motioning with her hands towards the food prepped and waiting to be taken next door.

"No, but thank you. I think everything is ready. In a while, I'll have Al and the girls walk the parade food over. No need for the BBQ food to go over until after the Baby Parade, as Michael and Wendy won't start the grill until then anyway."

"Then I'll just hang here, if that's okay, Suzanne," Al said, starting to move toward the living room area where Caela and Robin had taken seats.

"You are always welcome, Al."

"Thanks. I think there is too much togetherness at home. Jack won't sleep at all in his cot here. I think he doesn't like the way it smells. So, we're all up during the night when he cries. And with Stephen's folks here, it is just crowded and confusing. My mom is about ready to murder someone, anyone, I think. I'll stay here for a bit."

Al went over and squeezed in between the girls on the couch. They started talking about the day at the beach and what the other lifeguards would be doing that evening, since the lifeguards were off duty at 5:00 p.m. Then they could all head to a BBQ or picnic. The fireworks on the boardwalk would begin about 9:00 p.m.

Bill reflected on Al's admission of tension at his house. It happens in the best of families and on the best of vacations, he knew. Other than the tension over Catarina, their house party seemed to be going very smoothly.

Bill joined in the young people's conversation. "I hope it stays clear for the fireworks. I heard there is a chance of poor weather tomorrow. I hope it doesn't come too quickly and spoil tonight."

"Nah, it will stay fine for tonight. I predict rain mid-afternoon tomorrow, then because of the full moon and tide, we'll get that street flooding tomorrow night. Then it all drains away in a day or so. When you have been at the shore as many summers as I have, you get a feel for the weather changes and what to expect," Al said.

"Hmph," Catarina said obviously not sharing Al's excitement over the prospect of fireworks and fun on the boardwalk with his new, young girl friends.

Shelly Young Bell

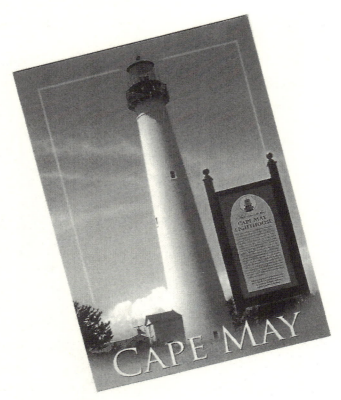

Dear Jenn,

Poor beach day today so we drove down to Cape May. Beautiful Victorian village by the sea, interesting history, restaurants and gift shops. They have "Cape May Diamonds" here – pure quartz stones washed down from up the Delaware River. Hate to admit it, but it has me thinking about diamonds!! Don't tell mom!!

Bill

Chapter 10

Morning, July 5th

There had been a dramatic change in the weather since the fireworks the night before. There was a little sun on the beach the next morning, but a much grayer sky partially hid it, and the sky increased in grayness as the day went on. Atlantic City to the north was barely visible through the fog. The sea was no longer a sapphire blue, but a fiery slate, churning and angry under the façade of normal waves, streaks of red-gold sun reflected across the gray surface as the sun struggled to be seen from behind the thickening clouds.

Ann felt it strongly. The emotion of the sea and air penetrated her physical being, and grasped her core. Ann had heard these sounds before, the unspoken pleas of the unknowing, the tide of emotions coming in and washing over her. Was it something already done? Was it something imminent? Would it be in the near future? These feelings never come over her without a reason, she had learned. All Ann could do was wait. Watch and wait.

"Mom?" Robin called out, trying to get her mother's attention, to yank Ann back to the reality of the morning from whatever this reverie was.

"Yes, Robin, what?"

"Al says that when the storm does come, they'll close the beach, you know, lighting and all that, and we were wondering, Caela and me, if maybe later we could do the boardwalk with Al and Roger, maybe get some pizza for supper, then do the amusements and rides."

"I see, well, some of us have decided to drive to Cape May later. You two don't want to join us?" Ann asked, full well knowing the answer.

"No. I mean, well, if we had a choice, I think we'd rather be up on the boardwalk, even if the weather might not be ideal."

"I know, with other young people having a good time, and not stuck in a car and having to endure a sit-down restaurant for dinner with us 'old' people," Ann said, teasing Robin a bit. Ann understood that a few hours on the boardwalk wouldn't do any harm. But still, this nagging feeling of alarm. . .

"Mom?"

"If Al promises to have you two back at the house safe and sound before we get back, then yes, okay. If the weather stays bad for the rest of the afternoon and evening, order pizza in and watch a movie. Che-Che and Catarina are staying behind, so you won't be alone. You can then go to the boardwalk another evening. We'll be 50 miles away, so the weather may not be the same for us down there. You'll have to decide what you do. Promise?"

"Yes, and thanks, mom!" Robin exclaimed and grabbed Ann's arm in excitement. She then turned and scampered off across the sand to Caela on her towel and Al sitting in the lifeguard chair.

There was a mist already in the air. The sun having been hidden by incoming clouds in just the few hours they'd been on the beach. Yes, it would rain. But would it be a long steady washout of a day or just a few showers or thunderstorms and then sudden sun again? Ann didn't know. Suzanne had indicated it would rain later, with flooding run-off, but they would wait and see what developed.

Suzanne had suggested a quiet morning, then after lunch, a caravan of whomever wanted to head to Cape May since it was not an ideal beach day. Very soon, Ann would head back to Diamond Dunes for a shower and to get dressed for some sightseeing, shopping and dinner out.

No one else from the house had come to the beach with Ann and the girls this morning. The weather, the excitement yesterday at the parade,

BBQ and fireworks had encouraged most of the others to have a slower start today. Although Suzanne had eventually joined them, sitting in her chair, talking with the group from Mike and Wendy's for a while.

Ann could feel the pounding of the ocean, the energy rising up through the sand and up her legs. It drew her to the sea; she did not want to miss an opportunity to be on the beach this week. She wondered for a moment if she and John should have moved to the coast when she retired from the Philadelphia Police Department. But no, with the old stone farmhouse in Buckelsmere and Robin's new school, these things were as they should be. She'd have to leave the beach and the sea for another time. Perhaps years down the road, but Ann could not deny the allure that living by the sea held for her.

Few people were on the beach this morning. They also must have decided the gray morning was not worth the effort to get ready to come for a short time and then return to their houses to get cleaned up and dressed. There was no guarantee the rain storm would hold off long enough to enjoy the beach and water once they did arrive.

Ann waved up the beach to Suzanne, knowing this morning was drawing to a close. She'd better get herself back up out of the cold water and return with Suzanne and the girls to the house. Suzanne was ready to leave, having given her hat to Marie, Stephen's mother. Marie was going to stay at the beach as long as she could that day, hopeful that the sun would come back out. After having sat with Marie and the others for an hour or so, Suzanne was ready to leave their group as she could now see exactly what Al had mentioned yesterday. Tensions were a bit high. It made her think of Ben Franklin's saying about guests and fish stinking after three days. There did seem that there had been enough together time and perhaps the house just wasn't large enough for so many people for an extended stay. Suzanne hoped Wendy wasn't tempted to solve the problem with a kitchen knife! Suzanne was so happy that the only bad fish at her house, this Catarina person, was not someone she'd have to endure for long nor in the future. She'd see to that when the goodbyes were said.

Suzanne reflected on the fact that it seemed her houseguests had all fallen into a very friendly companionship with each other this week without feeling cramped or put upon. Maybe the diversity of her houseguests lent itself to that – their wide range of ages and interests proving an asset to conversation rather than a hinderance to pleasantness.

Carl was there on the beach. He was walking up and down, back and forth, occasionally picking things out of the little basket and either tossing them back into the sand or putting them in a small cloth bag looped onto his belt, presumably things of value – coins, jewelry. Ann paid him little notice as she walked up the beach to where Suzanne was, careful not to step on broken shells or litter in her bare feet.

Carl watched the little group of friends all sitting together near the lifeguard stand, particularly the one with the large red sunhat. She was the one that Catarina had pointed out before. The one who allegedly knew where this 'treasure' was hidden that Catarina kept going on and on about.

A smiled crossed his face. Treasure. If there was any treasure, it wasn't here in Ocean City at her beach house. Catarina was wrong about that. If he pressed this woman, Suzanne, for the whereabouts of any treasure, what would be the outcome, would she tell him? Would she scream bloody hell and have the police on his doorstep? No, he'd have to take care of her in his own special way. No one would be any the wiser. He was no novice to the art of persuasion – physical and otherwise. Suzanne would tell him, and then? Well, Catarina would be out of luck if she thought he was sharing anything with her. Stupid, ridiculous woman. It would be all his. He'd be gone off to new beaches, new sunrises, new possibilities before she even realized it.

Carl walked up and down the beach in a weaving motion so that he could keep his eye on Suzanne, hidden beneath that red sunhat. She sat for a long time with the group of people on the beach, well past midday when her friends left and she stayed there alone. His stomach was growling for food. He'd wait. He'd enjoy a large roast beef and swiss cheese hoagie later. She stayed well past the sun having been hidden beneath a solid layer of gray clouds. Would she ever give it up and head home? He needed to get her alone and out of sight of any passers-by.

Finally, when the afternoon became sullen, damp and gusty with the storm blowing in from the ocean, he saw Suzanne leaving the beach, chair and towel in hand. The lifeguards blew their whistles and announced that because lightning had been spotted, they were closing the beach for the rest of the afternoon. Carl headed up to the boardwalk himself. He'd wait and follow her, hoping for his chance.

Carl had an arrangement with the tourist gift shop at the corner that he could leave his detector in the corner of the shop if he needed to during the day. So, he ducked in, nodded to the proprietor, and stowed his detector, ear phones and scoop in the corner, mouthed "I'll be back" to the young lady at the cash register and began following Suzanne down the two blocks towards her house.

He followed Suzanne at a distance, keeping her in sight as she plodded on down the sidewalk.

Good, he thought to himself. She's alone. It might be daylight, but with the bad weather, there was no one about on the street. He followed her off the sidewalk to the parking area underneath her house and toward the door and staircase that led upstairs.

Moving quietly, yet quickly, Carl came up behind her, looping a long piece of electrical cord he always had handy on his belt around her neck, believing he'd give her a seriously good scare and he'd have his information in a jiffy. Carl pulled the cord tight across her throat just as she reached up to hang the large red sunhat on a hook near the door and staircase.

"What?!?!?!" she exclaimed in surprise.

"Listen up, lady. Tell me where the treasure is and I'll let you go."

"Please! You're hurting me!"

Carl pulled the cord tighter, careful to stay behind her, out of sight.

"Tell me and I'll let you go,' he snarled again quietly.

"I don't know anything about any treasure. I'm not --!"

"You will tell me, or else," Carl threatened, mad his threats had not already met with success.

"I can't breathe –"

"Tell me – where is the treasure? Here or in Pennsylvania?"

"I – I'm not –" And, just that suddenly, she went limp and started to drop to the pavement. Carl, now in a bit of panic, grabbed her and dragged her over to the large yellow inner tube that was a couple of feet away. He placed her on it and felt for a pulse. None.

Damn! This wasn't what was supposed to happen. He looked around quickly. No one to be seen. He took the big red hat off the hook and laid it over her face. He picked up the towel she'd dropped and covered her torso, and then turned and swiftly walked away. Back to the boardwalk to establish an alibi as best he could in case someone had seen him in the vicinity. He knew he had to try to remain calm, say nothing, and wait to see what would happen next.

That's when he saw one of those noisy lifeguards, the one that had just closed their section of the beach, sprinting down the sidewalk away from him towards the beach. So quickly that one of his flip flops flew up into the air and landed on the sidewalk, but the young man did not stop and return to pick it up. He gave a quick look back over his shoulder, saw Carl and kept running. Damn, Carl thought again. Probably the young man had seen too much. Now he'd have to deal with that, too.

Chapter 11

Later that day, Cape May. July 5

Ann stood where the beach met the parking lot at Sunset Beach, and stared out into the grayness of the Delaware Bay. The wind had picked up, but they had dodged the showers all afternoon. Now it seemed very likely that the rest of their day would be wet. 'Fresh' was what the wind would be called. A 'Fresh' breeze – constant, hair blowing back, but not strong enough to whip up tears in the eyes like the wind off the Scottish moors, or off the Loch. Ann recognized this feeling, this smell, this grayness. She was taken back to a place, a land far away and years before. This wind, this grayness, these whispers.

Overhead the wind whistled though the ropes of the flag pole. The wind in her ears, through the lines, over and around the chairs and tables on the screened porch of the café to her left, all sung a song of warning to her. That high, wavering whine – not just in the wind, but almost like voices singing. She had heard it before, long ago, at a bridge in Scotland where she had gone as a graduate student to study criminal methods, her thesis work being on "Holmesian Abduction vs the Hunch".

A sound wild enough to induce madness. Sirens? Mermaids? She didn't know. She was convinced she'd never really know, but she had witnessed what it could do to a man caught in its grip. Ann was rigid, knowing that something wicked and evil happening was inevitable and imminent. This place, this Thin Place, was pulling at her, edging her closer to the world and the energies beyond. But Ann resisted giving in to it here, this afternoon.

Ann had experienced the awe and terror that a Thin Place could induce in a person. The first one she encountered was in Scotland so many years ago. And since then, a few more times in her travels. There is a Celtic saying that goes 'heaven and earth are only three feet apart.' But in a Thin Place the distance is so much shorter. The wall between this physical world we live in and the spiritual world beyond is practically non-existent. This shore, this beach sucked Ann's thoughts away, time seemed nonexistent and unimportant. A bit disoriented and confused. she fought against it. Ann tried to relax and let the infinite, the other worldly energy flow to her and speak to her. No words, no language, but speak it would and inform, speak and transform. The power at this shore, this beach could unnerve her or it could strengthen her. It would all depend on Ann's willingness to be open and experience it beyond the scope of her normal senses. But today Ann was in no mood for it.

"Having a good time?" John asked as he came up behind her.

"Trying to," Ann answered, pulling herself back to the here and now. "Do you hear it?" She asked him.

John was quiet and thoughtful for a few minutes. He and Ann hadn't had much alone time these past few days. Not that it was a complaint, but he did feel a bit unconnected and out of touch with her. He listened, wondering just what she was hearing. He knew he never heard it when she asked, but he also knew she must actually be hearing something. It could be that as an aging male with its inevitable hearing loss, he just didn't or couldn't hear it. He suspected that he never would have been able to hear it. He was not attuned to it. While Ann could and often did hear these things, there was little chance he ever would. He never knew whether he should be glad or sad over that fact. Ann had tried to explain it adequately to him, but he had decided it was not of his experience, nor would it ever be, no matter how much he wanted to share Ann's feelings and distress.

"I hear the wind," he settled on saying.

Ann was glad he did not deny her, her senses, her hearings and her sightings. She knew he didn't have it, but he was brave and kind enough not to scoff and deny it was there.

"Something dark is coming. Not just the rain. Something dark. And soon. I hope I am wrong," Ann explained simply. She did not want to put a total damper on the afternoon's fun, so she turned, smiled at John, took his arm and give it a squeeze.

"Where are the others?"

"Bill went into that shell shop over there to find a few postcards. For some reason he is keen on postcards."

"His mom, no doubt," Ann confirmed.

"Okay. Well, he went in there. Suzanne headed to the comfort station over behind the hot dog stand. She'll be out, although I fear there might have been a longer line at the lady's room than she anticipated," John explained. Then after a few moments of silence added, "It's a little weird to think we're standing out here on this point, where the Atlantic Ocean meets the Delaware Bay. So isolated, so vulnerable."

"So dark, so stormy. I'll say it. It's interesting with the old concrete ship wrecked here and practically sunk now all the way. The constant wind, the sense of isolation here. I can only imagine how it felt a hundred or more years ago. Like being at the ends of the earth," Ann mused. She turned her back to the bay and faced up into the parking lot, the wind tossing her hair forward into her face and eyes.

"At least the wind keeps the biting flies away," John observed.

"And keeps the temperature cooler than even just back the 50 miles at Suzanne's house. A world of difference here. I wonder . . . "

"Don't," John interrupted. "The girls will be fine. They're fine. Probably on the boardwalk with their new friends, eating pizza, winning at skee ball, and riding the amusement rides," John said. "Better if you don't worry about them. Robin has a keen head on her shoulders. She won't let them get into any trouble. They'll be fine."

"Yes, I am sure you are right. I want you to be right," Ann said. Then in a slightly mocking tone, "Yes, they will be fine." Slowly they walked back from the beach arm in arm, through the half empty parking lot toward where John had parked the car earlier, after their afternoon ride from Ocean City, down Ocean Drive through all the different shore communities. The day was getting increasingly darker as it went on.

"It's been a nice afternoon, luckily no heavy rain yet, though that sky looks like it'll let loose soon. A good day to be off the beach and doing something a little bit different," John said, as they walked a short way to his Jeep. He hit the unlock button on his key fob. "I'll open it up before the others return," he explained.

"John, what do *you* think about it all? I've been so uneasy since the afternoon we arrived. I did not anticipate this Catarina character, nor the complication of lifeguards and now," she turned to look around to be sure she wasn't being overheard, "with Bill and Suzanne – I just don't know. I think I'm getting too old for all this intrigue."

John put his arms around her shoulders. "Oh yeah, you're too old. That's funny. No, it's just that what may have seemed like it would be a few days of relaxing fun, has turned into a revolving door event. A lot of players, a lot of comings and goings. I admit, it has been disorienting at times, and I do long for our quiet old house at home. But next week or the week after, we'll be missing all this. Even the bad weather today, I promise."

"Bill? Suzanne?" Ann asked him again.

"Bill is the most straightforward, pleasant man I may have ever met," John confided. "If he and Suzanne decide to give romance a go, I say good luck, and I do truly hope it works. Suzanne – not so sure about her on this. Is she ready? I haven't been sure all these years why she hasn't moved on. She's attractive, fun, self-reliant. I would have thought some man somewhere along the line would have snapped her up."

"She's never said. Never actually confided why. But the truth is that she's fine on her own; she knows it. Why rush into a relationship for the sake of being with someone? No, I think she's been smarter than that. Lonely at times, though; she must have been."

John knew Ann had been lonely when had he met her, so he could only assume she would be able to recognize it in her best friend. He would take a positive stand on this matter, since Ann had brought it up and he sensed her uneasiness.

"I think the two of them make a lovely couple. They seem to be comfortable and happy in each other's company. They are both relatively conservative in their lifestyles. I would welcome having Bill as a staple in our circle of friends. It might be a little more difficult if you both were still working at the Philadelphia Police Department, but that's over. He's working in Buckelsmere full time trying to fit in as a model local resident. You only work on the odd case with him now. So even if, and I don't mean to sound like I think it will come to this, even if they gave it a go and it didn't work out for them, I don't think it will jeopardize your working relationship with Bill. Though if it does work out, it will mean our having to find a new tenant for the gate house apartment!"

Ann chuckled thinking of that, trying to find a better or as least as good a tenant as Bill had been these last four months.

Chapter 12

That Same Night. July 5

Bill stood in line at the register with his postcards that he had finally located. He knew that even if he sent them tomorrow, he'd be home before anyone received the post cards. Oh well, he'd send them anyway. He liked to imagine the faces of the recipient when they looked through that day's mail and found a postcard from him.

He quite enjoyed thinking about the brief message that he'd write to each person. You couldn't get too many words on the back of a postcard. It was an exercise in brevity for him as a writer. How much could he relay in the fewest number of words. He'd bought four – one for his parents, one for his favorite sister, one for his three great aunts and one for himself. He'd put his on the refrigerator at home under a magnet and have a happy memory every time he looked at it.

The line was moving very slowly. Bill hoped that his friends had not grown impatient. He had not located any postcards on his few solo forays in Ocean City, and he had not found any on their brief stop at the Cape May Lighthouse. Time was running out, but this tacky little tourist shell shop had plenty, and he was seizing the opportunity to purchase them in case he found no others the rest of the week! He was able to pick out interesting ones from the multiple spinning racks in the store.

As he waited, Bill noticed a counter display featuring Cape May Diamond jewelry. He studied it. Not very expensive. Quartz set in silver or gold-filled rings, necklaces and earrings.

The Diamond Dunes Murders

Something clicked in Bill's mind. Earrings. Suzanne had lost an earring on the beach. Maybe he'd buy her a pair of these. Would she think it inappropriate? Too forward? Too tacky? But the thought of her wearing them, thinking of her as she put them on in the morning was too good a thought for him to ignore. Bill rotated the display, studying them. He needed something not too gawdy, but not too simple or little girlish. He finally decided on a pair, placing the post cards and the earrings with a card from the rack explaining about the Cape May Diamonds on the counter. He knew that Suzanne probably was familiar with them, but he included the little card just in case. He was extremely happy with his purchases and was still smiling to himself when it was his turn to pay.

Cape May Diamonds were obviously a tourist marketing gimmick. He looked at the little card. The Kechemeche Indians from the area had believed the stones possessed supernatural powers bringing success and good fortune. Bill hoped so, he so very much hoped so. The quartz stones originated at the northern reaches of the Delaware River and over the years were washed and tumbled the two hundred miles south to the Delaware Bay beaches, particularly Sunset Beach, where the stones would wash up onto the shore. Pretty enough, Bill thought, but not as sharp or bright as a real diamond. He hoped when Suzanne saw the earrings, she liked that he had chosen stones in their more natural rough form instead of having been cut to simulate their much more expensive quartz cousins.

Diamonds. Bill thought about that for a few breathless moments. Diamond Dunes. Cape May Diamonds. Diamonds. Seemed to be a theme. He wondered if it was a sign. But Bill felt that step would be far too premature. Good God, he hadn't even kissed the woman yet!

The cashier dropped the earrings, card, and postcards into a little brown bag. She took Bill's cash, made quick change, and with a brief, unfelt smile handed it to Bill and turned to the next customer.

Bill left the shop, smiling and planning. The other three were waiting by the Jeep. He walked over to it.

"Sorry, long line."

"No worries. It's a relaxed kind of afternoon," John said. "Suzanne, what about some supper. I saw a place, an Italian and Seafood type place, back in town, Grandmother's –"

"*God*mother's," Suzanne corrected him. "Yes," she added, checking her watch. "Just about right for drinks and an Early Bird dinner. Are we too young for that? Do we have to be senior citizens for that?" she asked, half in jest, have in earnest.

"I think they'll seat and feed us, no matter how old we are," Ann assured her. "I hadn't realized tooling around looking at shore resorts and historic sites could make me so hungry. John, let's go."

"John, follow this street straight back up into Cape May village proper. We can't miss it. Sunset Boulevard becomes West Perry Street. The restaurant is right at that corner. Take the first parking space you see once we get up there. They do not have a parking lot, so we have to park on the street. I hope we can get find a spot. This crappy weather often drives all the beachgoers up onto the boardwalk and into the shops and eateries. The occasional bad weather day is good for the local businesses."

Once inside and seated, Bill took Ann's advice. After a quick perusal of the menu, he ordered a bottle of chilled Feudi Di San Gregorio Rubrato Aglianico, a plate of loaded garlic bread, and an antipasto plate for the table to share while they studied the menu for their entrees.

As the others chatted over the selections, Bill thought about all he had seen today in such a short time. He could understand the allure that The Shore had on people, and why they kept coming back again and again. Suzanne not only had shown them all a wonderful week of hospitality, but today had shown them the expanse and diversity of shore communities. She talked a little about the history of the New Jersey barrier islands from the earliest Native American settlements, long before the explorer Henry Hudson had sailed past on his way to the New York City area, through the Revolutionary War and into the 20th Century. This area, Cape May, had played such an important part during World War II. Bill had picked up a leaflet to take back to Che-Che. He had found it so interesting that he had read it during the ride. Through use of lookout towers and gun emplacements, the U.S. military guarded the entrance to the Delaware Bay. There were two Navy bases that trained and guarded the area. World War II history was becoming a new interest of his, Bill realized. Perhaps he could set one of his murder mysteries during that time period, which would give him the opportunity to do research into the era.

The waiter approached them for their dinner order. Even after sharing the appetizers and the wine, Bill was still hungry and ready for dinner. He ordered the linguini and clams. Ann had the risotto del giorno (crab and asparagus as it turned out). John ordered his standard Italian favorite, veal parmesan, and Suzanne settled on the three-cheese ravioli.

Just finishing the last of their platters, with Bill contemplating the choice of cannoli versus limoncello cake, Ann's cell phone vibrated on the table.

"Sorry," Ann said, picking it up to see who it might be. Everyone knew it could be only one person. Robin.

"Mom, I think you need to come home. Right now!" Robin said. The quaver in her voice was alarming.

"What?" Ann asked.

"It's Suzanne, she's dead!"

Ann looked up and into Suzanne's eyes.

"What? Say that again," Ann asked Robin, trying to remain calm.

"It's Suzanne, she's been murdered!" Robin cried.

"Robin, honey, Suzanne is sitting right here next to me."

"Mom, come! Please!"

Chapter 13

Evening, July 5

There was no dessert that night. When he realized what was happening back in Ocean City, Bill rose and hurriedly made the hostess ring up their tab so he could pay it, while John left to go get the car and bring it around to the front door. Suzanne tried comforting Ann, as Ann was having difficulty staying calm. After all, Robin was involved.

Obviously, something very bad had happened back in Ocean City at Suzanne's house. And here they were, fifty miles away, in the dark, in the rain, and facing a difficult drive back. Ann knew she should take comfort in the fact that before hanging up, Robin did assure her that she and Caela were alright. 100% okay and safe.

Suzanne, alarmed that people thought she had been murdered, decided to call Che-Che's cell phone. No one had Catarina's phone number. No one had thought to ask Catarina for it since she seemed to be constantly underfoot. Suzanne and Ann quickly climbed into the back seat as Suzanne was having a brief conversation with Che-Che. Che-Che wasted no time getting off the phone to get downstairs to see what was happening.

"Che-Che knows nothing. She is headed downstairs to see what is going on. She had been working on the computer, expecting the girls home soon as the rain had started, and their curfew was fast approaching. Catarina was there, too, watching a program on the TV, so she also was unaware anything was happening out on the street below them," Suzanne updated them as they buckled their seat belts.

Bill asked John. "Do you want me to drive?"

John looked at him and shook his head. "No, but thanks. I've been waiting years to be able to do this. This is not exactly Kojak's 'cherry' police light, but it'll do, I hope. GPS says 29 minutes, light traffic. I bet with this I can get there in 20. Hold on!" John said as he pulled a metal bar out of the glove compartment, plugged it into the cigarette lighter, and switched it on. Instant red, white and blue flashing police lights were now on the dashboard pointing out forward, hopefully to help clear the way for a much faster trip back to Suzanne's house.

It took twenty-two hair raising minutes in the end. John took the Garden State Parkway north from Cape May to Somers Point, but even with his flashing police bar light, traffic was slower than he wanted to go. Out onto the barrier island there were whole areas under water. Luckily the Jeep had excellent clearance and they pressed on ahead through the flooding until a block from Diamond Dunes. Here, there were a great many other vehicles blocking the way – police, fire, ambulances – all with their own flashing lights. A local cop motioned for them to stop.

"Can I help you?"

"Yes, officer," Bill answered, pulling out his police identification, "Police – and we have the owner of the house where the incident happened, someone whom you may suspect is the victim, Suzanne Beck."

The young officer's face showed extreme interest, and he spoke quickly into his walkie-talkie to senior police members. He waved John through, telling him to continue driving as far as he could. When the road was too clogged with official vehicles to proceed, John pulled the Jeep up into someone's driveway so they could all get out without stepping down into a puddle six inches deep. He would come back and move it as soon as he was able to get it closer to Diamond Dunes.

Shoes in hand, they waded through the water towards Diamond Dunes, where it was the obvious epicenter of the action. As they approached, Ann called out, "Robin! Robin!". Ann couldn't see her anywhere, but she knew that Robin had to be there somewhere.

"Ann, over here," they could hear Che-Che calling back, from where the sidewalk should be, but closer to Michael and Wendy's house. She was there with Robin and Caela under a large golf umbrella, standing in the water, watching.

Robin and Ann hugged, Ann making sure Robin was indeed okay before turning to Caela to check on her as well.

"Mom, you were right. It wasn't Suzanne. Thank God, Suzanne, it wasn't you," Robin said, tears coming quickly now at the enormity of the situation. "It turned out that it was Marie – Stephen's mom. You know, Stephen is married to Kathy, Michael's daughter. We were mistaken in the dark and rain and all."

"I came down as soon as Suzanne called," Che-Che explained. "I found Robin, Caela and Al down here under your house, standing in the middle of the flooded car park area. They were looking at that big yellow tube thing, adrift on the water all by itself, adrift and floating out to the street. On it was a body, a woman, wearing your big red sun hat, Suzanne, drawn up over her face, and a beach towel draped over the rest of her. No wonder Robin thought it was you. Al ran next door to call the police, only to learn that Marie had been missing for several hours. She had not returned home from the beach late that afternoon as expected."

Suzanne took up the story, "So she must have come home, came to my house to drop off the hat that I loaned her this morning, and something happened, someone killed her," Suanne looked at Che-Che's face in the flashing police lights through the rain trying to ask the question no one wanted to ask. Che-Che had been expecting it.

"No. Both Catarina and I had spent the entire afternoon, suppertime and early evening upstairs within sight of each other. So – no," was all Che-Che would say, but finally did add, "and since here, under your house, is now a crime scene, they won't let us back upstairs yet. Next door is in total chaos once they were informed that Marie had been killed, so I'm not taking the girls over there. And I don't know any of the other neighbors. I don't know where would be safe, who *isn't* the killer!"

Bill and John joined the others where they stood. They had been talking with the Ocean City Police Criminal Investigations Division Detective Chapman who had arrived and had taken over the investigation.

Bill spoke. "Definitely Marie. Definitely murder. Maybe strangulation -- there are indications of that, but maybe it was a heart attack, but that would not explain her odd placement on the inner tube with the hat over her face and the towel over her torso. The Medical Examiner is on his way now, but the flooding is hampering everything. They will take the girls' statements soon, now that there is a parent and chaperone here."

"Damn straight. I wouldn't let those policemen talk with these youngsters without a proper adult here!! I've seen way too many TV shows to know better than that! Next thing we'd know is that they'd charge these two with murder!" Che-Che blurted out. Bill tried hard not to smile at her protective ferocity, her impersonation of a mother tiger.

"Yes, well, they did find the body. It will be very straight forward. Once the police check that they had supper on the boardwalk and time the walk back here, their alibi, hate to call it that, will hold up solid." Bill continued, "I have asked that they let our group head upstairs out of the weather. The chief says just as soon as the medical examiner arrives and studies the scene, they will allow that. Then, dry clothes, hot drinks, and the girl's statements." He turned towards Ann, "Ma-am, a word?" Ma-am. Bill hadn't called her that all week, reserving its use for purely work-related conversations.

"Okay. Robin, are you okay to stay here with John, Suzanne and Che-Che?"

"Yes, I'm okay now. Now that you're back and Suzanne is okay. Caela and I, we're ready to talk to the Detective, too, if they want," Robin assured Ann; Caela nodding her consent.

Ann nodded, "We'll see." Ann and Bill sloshed through the water towards the flooded parking area under Diamond Dunes. Bill pointed to the area where the yellow inner tube would normally be stored.

"He must have killed Marie here, dropped her onto the inner tube and covered her with Suzanne's hat and a towel that were handy and nearby. When it flooded down here, the inner tube floated out towards the street. The local police know that probably no evidence is left here as a result, but they will be checking everything when the tide recedes as much as it is going to. Low tide is about midnight. They request that we stay put, stay here, until interviews are done, and any additional forensic gathering is completed overnight or tomorrow.

"I suggest we let them talk with Robin and Caela now – let that be over with. The girls will sleep better knowing they will not have to face it later or in the morning."

"I agree," Ann said.

Bill continued. "I ran upstairs quickly. Catarina seems terribly agitated and upset. I don't know if she needs a sedative or just a strong drink. She confirmed what Che-Che had already told us. Neither Catarina nor Che-Che saw or heard anything after the girls left with Al for supper on the boardwalk about 4:00 p.m.. Catarina watched TV mostly, Che-Che was absorbed in something on her laptop. It was stormy. They had the windows closed, so I am not surprised they heard nothing.

"Detective Chapman let me know that Marie's jewelry was taken – her rings, her necklaces, not her earrings though as they were just plastic hoops. Perhaps that is all this is really – an opportunistic theft."

"In broad daylight?"

"I know. It's a stretch. I just don't want to consider the other possibility. That the intended victim was Suzanne," Bill said quietly.

"Yes. Someone mistook Marie for Suzanne. Similar build and hair color, Marie was wearing Suzanne's hat and came here to Suzanne's house. I think we do have to consider that possibility and relay it to the Detective. He will want to interview Suzanne a little more thoroughly as a result. Can't be helped. Bill, don't worry. I am sure when it all comes to light, there's no reason in the world that someone would be targeting Suzanne. I've known her for twenty years. Other than a little jewelry, some nice designer clothes and her two houses, Suzanne owns little. She is not extravagant or showy, or has anything that would warrant being stalked and murdered. Let's just take this calmly and slowly. Let's let the local police force do their thing. I don't think there's anything we can contribute at this point other than that Marie was here returning a sun hat. And let's hope that's all the connection there is, that neither she nor Suzanne was the intended victim, that this was just a random robbery turned deadly."

"What do you think we ought to let Suzanne know now, in advance of her interview?"

"I hate to muddy any waters and make it look like we are either stepping in where we haven't been asked yet, or obstructing the local investigation by letting information be leaked that shouldn't be shared yet."

Bill and Ann waded slowly back through the dark water toward the others. Detective Chapman was talking with Suzanne, who was standing with her hand over her mouth, as if in horror. The Detective was a man in his late 50's, Ann thought. Gray hair, well-tanned, a kindness around his blue eyes, but with the expected police briskness of getting the job done efficiently and quickly.

"Oh, my, no," Suzanne said to him, "Marie was probably here to return the sun hat – the large red sun hat – I lent to her this morning when I left the beach. She had forgotten hers, and was ever hopeful that the sun would come out. We were all sitting together, talking, and when I got up to leave, about 11-ish, I left my hat with her. She was going to stay on the beach as long as the weather held out, so most of the afternoon, I guess."

Bill and Ann joined them. Al popped back out of his front door and came over to them.

"Al, I am so sorry about Marie," Suzanne said.

"Thanks. Of course, I barely knew her. She was Kathy's mother in law. I rarely saw them. I just had to get out of there for a bit. There's a policeman in there with Rob, Marie's husband, but he won't be much help. He had been inside all day, as his bad back and neck doesn't let him do a lot of walking around. He never once went to the beach. We were lucky he came out to see Jack in the Baby Parade. So, no way he killed her and lifted her onto that inner tube. Dad and Mom are trying to sooth it all over but really, how can they? Murder! Jesus!" Al said. Caela stepped closer to him and asked, "What can we do?"

"Nothing. I just needed to *not* be in the middle of the scene playing out at home. Poor Kathy and Stephen, juggling their little guy, Jack, who is crying and upset, and he doesn't even know why. Stephen looks shocked, 'in shock' rather, so pale and quiet. I'm thinking someone ought to call a medical person to come over, but I don't know. I don't even know if the cops would let someone in."

Caela said to him, "On TV they always offer a blanket and a hot drink, maybe you could do that?" Ann had to smile, in spite of the seriousness of the situation. Caela must watch cop shows on TV.

"John, will you ask one of the Medical guys if he will go over just to check on Stephen and Rob as well?" Ann asked.

"Sure. I'll be right back."

Al continued, "Dad is in control, marshalling everyone around, out of the way of the police talking with Rob. I am not sure why they are so interested in talking with him, he clearly knows nothing."

Ann glanced at Bill. Neither dared say it. Most murders are committed by someone known to the victim. That category of suspect usually has the most motive and opportunity. The police would be very thorough in their interviewing process, and the constructing of the timeline of where and when everyone connected with Marie had been. They didn't want to cast any suspicion on Rob, yet they didn't want to mention that he'd probably had nothing to do with this. Marie's jewelry had been stolen. Rob would not have stolen his own wife's jewelry. Ann and Bill knew they had to leave the release of information and details to the Ocean City Police Department's discretion. No telling what detail might be the critical one.

The Diamond Dunes Murders

Ann and Bill knew this from their years of experience, and years of fearing that critical information falling into the perpetrator's hands might allow him to adjust his story and actions, thus being able to avoid detection.

Ann knew that Al, Caela, and Robin were not the murderers. She knew that Che-Che and Catarina had each other as rock solid alibis. She suspected that Michael and Wendy, Stephen, Kathy and Rob had nothing to do with it, as they had all pretty much been under each other's feet all afternoon at their house – as bad weather had kept them in during the afternoon. It had been Tour de France on TV, self-serve lunch during late mid-day, reading and napping in the afternoon to stay quiet during Jack's nap. Marie obviously had left the family group and stayed on the beach for the rest of the afternoon on her own when the others had returned to the house at lunchtime. She had told Suzanne that she came for beach time and would get as much as she could even though it was a far from perfect day for it.

Based on that, the rest of the extended family next door had no idea when she might return. There was no concern over her absence until suppertime, after Al had gone to the boardwalk with the girls, probably hours after Marie had returned and been murdered under Diamond Dunes. Ann could see the strain in Al, having faced the fact that there had been a dead body there, just feet away around the corner from the staircase that he and the girls had come down to head out for an evening of fun.

Al explained that Stephen had walked back to the beach about six o'clock, looking for Marie, but the rain started and no one was left on the beach at that point, so he returned home. At seven o'clock they called the police who told them to sit tight and stay off their phones in case she tried to call them. Often these things resolved themselves within a few hours. At eight o'clock, Al and Robin and Caela had walked home in the rain, laughing and joking with each other, the rising flood tide and rain runoff just part of their fun. In the storm and dark, it had struck them as just bad luck that the yellow inner tube had floated out from underneath Suzanne's house – Caela saying she obviously hadn't realized she needed to tie it up!

They approached it to secure it again against floating away when they realized that someone was on it – floating on it, silent and motionless.

Ann could see Al was in a state of total distress. Al looked at Suzanne, everyone looked at Suzanne. "We thought it was you – hat, towel, under your house, on your floaty thing. So . . . I ran into my house and had dad call the police. By the time I got back out here to Caela and Robin, it was only a few minutes before we saw police lights approaching. The flooding has gone down a bit since then. It just was so bizarre. I can't get that image out of my mind."

"You will," Bill assured him. "Just give it time. Focus on other images, like the fun you had tonight on the boardwalk. It gets easier."

Al swallowed and nodded his thanks to Bill.

"There's nothing I can do to help at home, so I thought I'd come out here and stand with you all. I'm sure you could all come in – "

"No thanks, Al, I think we would just add to the confusion and . . . not do any of us any good, if you get me," Ann said. She put her hand on Al's shoulder. Although he was eighteen and legally grown up, finding a murder victim, well – that would be a shock to even the most stalwart.

The hours dragged on. Marie's body was taken away and the medical examiner and his team finished their part of the investigation. It had been long enough that it was low tide and the flooding had receded back to the bay, awaiting the next high tide.

It was after midnight when Detective Chapman spoke quietly to Suzanne, who nodded, and then he waved the group towards the staircase and allowed them to ascend the stairs. Caela and Robin's statements were taken, with Suzanne and Ann standing with them. They could really add nothing to the pool of facts he had already gleaned from Al. They were on the boardwalk with Al for supper, playing the odd game, riding a couple of indoor rides that were operating in spite of the weather. Yes, they were sure that the pizza parlor and the game operators would remember their having been there. Because of the weather, the boardwalk was pretty deserted, so the pizza place had been almost empty, and the games and rides pretty much unattended. They walked back about eight o'clock, sandals in hand, as the flooding on the street reached all the way up their block by then. When they arrived home, that is when they saw the body floating on the yellow inner tube, red sun hat over the face, and ocean blue towel over the legs and body. They had thought it was Suzanne because it was her hat and inner tube. Then Al ran for help. They stood in one spot until the first patrol car arrived. No, they had not touched the body, or anything. Just stood in the dark, in the flood waters, waiting. No, they had not gone upstairs. Robin knew not to touch anything or do anything to disturb a crime scene. Che-Che and Catarina had been alerted when Suzanne had called them. Then Che-Che had come downstairs at once, just as the police were arriving. It all seemed to have happened so fast.

The detective really hadn't expected much else. He knew that they were just kids having a good time at the shore, as kids always did. He gave Ann and Suzanne a sympathetic look and explained that his men would still be there for a while, and that they may need to speak to Suzanne again, as home owner, and perhaps as intended victim.

Suzanne cringed. How could that be? She had no enemies, she owned nothing worth killing for. She looked at Ann, hoping to see an answer in Ann's face, but was disappointed. Suzanne knew they were all thinking it. Marie was mistaken for Suzanne, and now she's dead.

"Come on, every one, up we go. Dry clothes, and something to lessen the shakes," Suzanne suggested.

The rain let up; the flooding receded as predicted. But the lightning continued on into the night. The breeze was stiff enough that they left the windows closed against it. The wind's voice was loud in Ann's ears. Yes, she told it, yes, she had heard and was aware of the crime committed here. Yes, she'd be watchful and make sure it was put right, as best she could. Ann just wanted the wind and the voices to calm down, so she could sleep, then rise in the morning to think and start the healing process that so many of them needed.

Chapter 14

Morning, July 6

Al had lain in bed for what was left of the night, restless, unable to sleep. He was due at work that next morning, so the closer it got to the alarm going off, the more impossible it seemed he would get to sleep. The image of Marie floating, drifting around under Suzanne's house stayed in his mind and was ever more vivid if he closed his eyes. He left the light on and tried sitting up in bed, to keep that image as far away as possible.

He wondered how Robin and especially Caela were doing. They were younger than he. He had been surprised by their strength and courage during the whole police ordeal. But Robin's mom and that man, Bill, they were cops after all. Robin probably had had experience with this before.

Caela was a revelation to him. So pretty and funny. She made laughing and doing the simplest thing so much fun. He didn't feel awkward when she was around. But she was only fourteen. Really too young to be serious about. Probably. Well, maybe not. He still had two days to hang out with her. Then there was the internet. He planned to ask Suzanne to be sure to invite Caela back to the shore house again. He was sure Suzanne would do that for him, as Robin and her parents usually came several times over the summer.

Al had thought the stress he was already feeling this summer was about as bad as it could get. Then this. He felt like he'd explode if anything else happened and involved him. It was only the first week of July; summer was only three weeks old. He had managed to graduate high school. Just. Without excellent grades and not much interest in school, he had slogged through the four years. Band had been his primary interest. But as his father pointed out there was little future in that. All Fall term his folks had pressured him into selecting a college, one that they approved of. He finally decided a local one would do as well as any other. He applied late and was surprised to hear back from Temple University in Philadelphia that they had accepted him into their Music School. His mom was well pleased because that was where she had gotten her Master's Degree. But college! He had no idea how would he fare. But he *could* take the train from Temple University station directly to the station in Buckelsmere, that he did know. Finally, a positive thought. He'd nurture that thought for a while.

The alarm went off loudly. Al pulled himself out of a bad dream he could not remember upon waking. The lamp was on, he was still sitting up but slumped over a bit. So, he *had* eventually fallen asleep. But now he felt awful, drugged almost, from the lack of sleep and the shock of last night. Just something else he would have to push through.

What would the rest of the household be like today? He dreaded to think, but he knew he had to get ready, grab some toast or something, and get to his lifeguard post. They would not need him underfoot here today and being there at the house was the last thing Al wanted.

Whatever arrangements Rob and the others had to take care of, Al would leave to all of them to deal with. He just felt he had to get out of the house and away from them all before the blackness in his head totally took over.

Al munched his cinnamon toast as he went up the sidewalk for the beach and the lifeguard stand. He'd planned to box Roger about the ears a bit for not showing up last night, but he really ought to thank him. As a result of Roger not showing up, Al had been alone with Robin and Caela, and had a wonderful time as the only guy with them. No one to share them with, no one against whom to compete for their attention.

The tides and street flooding had receded. Everything was still very wet and disheveled. There on the sidewalk ahead of him, a flip-flop, just like the kind Roger always wore. A strange brand, and with a neon green stripe around the sole. Al picked it up, wondering if Roger had lost it or if it were someone else's. He'd take it to Roger and ask. If it wasn't Roger's, he could leave it at the top of the stairs from the street to the boardwalk where its owner would eventually see it. Everyone from their street accessed the beach via that staircase and portion of the boardwalk.

Roger was already at his station, in the lifeguard chair. Al was surprised and looked at his watch. 8:35 a.m. Early for Roger. Duty didn't start until 9:00 a.m. Al walked closer to the lifeguard chair. Seagulls circled overhead, calling to one another. One broke away from the others and dropped closer to Roger, then actually landed on the arm of the white wooden chair. Roger didn't move, didn't even look at the bird. He just kept looking out to sea.

"Roger, who's your friend?" Al called out. He got no reply. Al was still twenty feet or so away from the chair and Roger. Something deep inside him warned him not to go any closer. A second seagull landed on the chair and slowly reached out to peck at Roger's arm. Roger didn't react.

Al felt the blood drain from his head and arms. He felt like ice in the warm morning July sun, unable to move as he watched. He dropped the flip-flop, dropped his lifeguard bag, and stood there watching the seagulls decide if Roger was breakfast or not.

Roger was obviously dead.

The next hour was a blur for Al. The same police detective arrived and talked to Al, who hazily recounted his overnight hours and morning's activities, and his finding Roger's body. Al knew this probably made him the prime suspect. But he had no motive, and was not sure how Roger had died. Maybe it wasn't murder? There had been a lot of lightening during the night after the rain had ended. Maybe it was just a horrible accident.

The Diamond Dunes Murders

It had been so horrifying to see Roger like that, dead, sitting up and staring out to sea. As if nothing was wrong. Al needed help, Detective Chapman decided, so he called Michael's number and asked that Michael and Wendy come at once to the beach to fetch Al.

When Michael and Wendy did arrive minutes later, hurrying across the sand, they had an entourage with them: Suzanne, Ann, Bill, the two teenage girls, Che-Che, Catarina and Kathy. Turned out that Suzanne had run out early for breakfast donuts and cheese Danish, and a carafe of coffee to take next door to help out, so the two households had been together when the Detective's call had gone through to Michael's phone.

Caela suggested they should go back to Diamond Dunes, pack their bags and head home. Immediately. Ann and Bill weren't as anxious to do that as the younger ones were.

"Robin," Ann asked as they stood in the sand a good hundred feet from the lifeguard chair in the bright July sunlight, "tell me what you see."

Robin was none too keen on the idea, but Robin knew that tone in her mother's voice. She was not going to take No for an answer. Caela looked at Robin in horror, afraid she'd be next on the list of interviewees again.

"Well, what do you see? Tell me everything."

"Okay. Let's see," Robin said, taking a look up and down the beach from where they stood. "The lifeguard's chair, empty now, of course. Yellow police tape all over and around it. A small, curious crowd is still standing there, I suppose wondering what has happened. Maybe ten people or so, a few adults but mostly kids. A few family groups further up the beach and little kids in the water. Maybe five, six groups there. Three guys surfing, the waves left over from the storm last night.

"And down the beach, the other way?" Ann asked gently.

"Nothing much. Nothing out of the ordinary. There are six seagulls down beach a bit, looking at us. I swear they are looking at us! Further down there are people in the water, and some on their towels laying in the sun."

"That's it?"

"Yeah, I think so. Why? What are we looking for?"

"My dear Robin, it's not what is here, it's what is *not* here that I am finding so interesting"

"I thought the police said Roger had probably been struck by lightning," Robin said, fearing her mother's police instincts were starting to work overtime.

"That's what they may have said, but I don't believe that is what really happened. At least not the whole story. Come on, guide me off the sand, out of the bright sun and back to the house. I need to make a phone call."

Robin and Caela didn't have to be asked twice. Michael and his family had already left, taking poor Al home to have a quiet lie-down, and some time to deal with his nerves after his discovering two bodies in less than twelve hours.

Catarina lingered, not leaving with Ann and the others. They would not even notice she was not with them until later, she figured. She'd explain she had stayed out in the sun, away from the confusion at the house next door, away from death and police interviews as she had nothing to do with any of this.

She'd say it, but she knew deep down inside that somehow, she did have something to do with this. Marie, probably. That young man, maybe. Oh, how she hoped her suspicions were wrong.

The others trooped up the sand, still wet on the surface from the rain last night. Eventually the sun would dry it all out, and it would be a lovely day, but not yet. Catarina looked up and down the beach but did not see Carl.

Where is that man? He might think he could hide, but she'd find him. In the end, all it took was asking another lifeguard about him, who pointed towards the surf shop at the end of the boardwalk, explaining Carl was often there. Catarina went up onto the boardwalk, brushing the wet sand off her feet and slipping on her flip-flops. The young clerk said that Carl had not been in yet that morning, but he had digs down at 4th Street. A small place, like a garage along there where he was spending the summer.

The Diamond Dunes Murders

Catarina marched off to 4th Street, several blocks away, screwing up her nerve and deciding on her tactics once she found him and confronted him.

But Catarina didn't get too far long before she saw Carl approaching her on the boardwalk. He pushed his way through the crowd outside the Surfing School storefront awaiting their instructor. He saw Catarina at the last minute and paused, not sure why she was here.

"A word, Carl," Catarina said, and motioned to the railing of the boardwalk. He went with her to the railing, away from the throng of walkers and bikers, still thick on the boardwalk mid-morning.

"Have you heard – Marie, the woman visiting next door, was killed last night?" Catarina started saying, her voice low but full of fury. Carl sneered at her. This pint sized nobody wasn't going to accuse him, not intimidate him.

"What of it?" he asked.

"Carl, she was killed under Suzanne's house. She had Suzanne's hat. The hat that I pointed out to you as something to recognize as belonging to Suzanne. I said 'press her'. Suzanne, not Marie! Tell me you didn't do this!"

"How was I to know she wasn't my target? She was wearing the hat; she went to the right house. She – "

"She NOTHING!" Catarina yelled. People started to stare. Catarina lowered her voice again, and tried to control herself. "Murder was never what I suggested. I said 'press her', see if we could find out what she had done with Aldo's treasure."

"I tried. She wouldn't answer me. I started to try to keep her from screaming for help and somehow – well – then she was dead."

"You fool, you absolute fool. I want nothing to do with this nor with you! Stay away from me; far, far away!"

"You be careful, missy. Don't threaten me or you'll – "

"I'll what? Be next? Not hardly."

"That's what that lifeguard said, and look what that got him," Carl snarled at her.

"Lifeguard? You killed that poor young man, too?"

"Well, yes, stupid boy. He saw me with that woman, Marie. He saw far too much. So, I followed him, caught up with him, convinced him to come down to my place for a talk, and eventually, well, you can imagine how that ended."

Catarina heard all this with increasing horror, her skin crawling, her stomach churning. She had to get away from this madman. Even she wouldn't have stooped to murder, not even for what she believed was at stake. She needed to escape him. She thought she could. He didn't know who she really was, not really. Catarina took one last look at his jeering face, turned and walked quickly back up the boardwalk. She'd pack and leave. No treasure, but she'd be free from this lunatic and any involvement in his eventual take down. Catarina was not naïve enough to think that the police would not piece it together. Time was not in her favor at this point and she must get away.

Chapter 15

Afternoon, July 6

Robin noticed that things were happening way too quickly back at the house. Bill was on his cell phone and directing Che-Che with her laptop to do research. Her mom was on *her* cell phone and writing a few notes as she listened to whomever was at the other end of the line. Catarina had been gone a while, but when she did return, refused the offer of lunch, which had been assigned to Robin and Caela to coordinate and dish out to everyone. Catarina hurried to her cot area and started packing. She was leaving, thanks for the hospitality but two murders were two too many, she explained. John provided support where he could, offering iced tea or Cokes, and trying to stay out of the way.

Robin wondered how Al and the neighbors were all doing, but knew she needed to keep her focus here, at Suzanne's house. Suzanne seemed totally preoccupied. Not involved in whatever urgent activity it was that the others were doing. She seemed disturbed, thoughtful, a crease of worry across her forehead. Whatever it was, she did not share it. Perhaps she did not want to burden the others. But if Suzanne had been the intended victim, no wonder she was acting a bit out of it, Robin thought.

Robin could see her lovely week at the shore completely falling apart at this point. Caela wouldn't want to go back to the beach ever again. Al was in no shape to hang out with them today, and probably not tomorrow. Catarina was leaving in a panic. Yes, Robin thought, panic was how she'd describe Catarina's response. She looked over at her mom. Had her mom picked up on that? Had Bill? She needed to be sure her mom and Bill had noticed it as well, but without upsetting Suzanne any further, without making Catarina leave even more quickly. Maybe she was all wrong, but she was pretty sure she had heard Catarina say *two* murders.' What made her think the second one was murder? Earlier, the police had been suggesting lightning had killed Roger.

It was about two in the afternoon when Detective Chapman arrived again. The entire group sat around in the living area and on the stools at the kitchen island. Catarina was still there, having packed, but not having actually gotten out the door yet.

"Medical Examiner says the young man died by electrocution. At first glance it would indicate a lightning strike, but that doesn't explain why there is no sign of that on the lifeguard chair. These things aren't an exact science. Weird things do happen, in unexplainable ways. There were burns on his hands, but nothing else. Death was about six last night, so I am assuming that the alibis you all provided last night for Marie's death hold for this death as well, not that we're saying that anyone needs an alibi for the lifeguard's death. We'll know more later. Until then, please everyone should stay here, locally, and I'll be checking in again with you soon," the detective said.

"What?! Stay here?! I was planning on heading home today!" Catarina gasped.

"No, sorry, I may need to ask more questions," Detective Chapman explained.

Ann and Bill slowly turned to each other and exchanged a glance. Robin noticed that glance. The game was afoot, as they say. Robin knew this is where it all got interesting. This was the point that her mom and Bill would interject themselves. She waited for it. But there was silence. Had she misread it, Robin wondered?

The detective spoke again as he rose, "Mrs. Essex and Detective Dancer – perhaps a word downstairs, in private, on my way out?"

The Diamond Dunes Murders

"Bingo," Robin said underneath her breath, to herself, with satisfaction that she had been right.

"We have a man at the station," Detective Chapman started, once the three of them had reached the parking area under the house and had securely shut the door behind them. "The police had been called by several concerned citizens on the boardwalk late this morning that he was being aggressive and was threatening a woman. A woman with an eye patch. By the time my patrol man reached the scene, the woman had walked off, but we brought this man in, to be on the safe side," Detective Chapman paused.

Ann knew he was deciding how much he should share with them. So, she and Bill waited. Often silence was the best encouragement.

"After your phone calls this morning and early afternoon, and after the information you shared with me, I made a few phone calls to the Philly Police Department and to the Buckelsmere Police Department. Yes, I checked you out –"

"As well you should have," Bill agreed.

"Yes, well, you are who you say you are. You do have quite a reputation back home for solving cases, even those not in your jurisdiction. I have no trouble with that. Lord knows if we can wrap this up quickly, all the better, even if OCPD has had help. The young lifeguard was electrocuted, but we don't believe by lightening, sitting in that chair as he was found. It happened much earlier and the body was then placed there overnight. Your call to me about the man with the metal detector was enlightening, because you see –"

"You have him in custody, already, don't you, Detective?" Ann asked.

"Yes. Same man who was threatening the woman on the boardwalk. His name is Carl Green. We were about to release him after the boardwalk threatening incident when you called us. Normally we would have just released him with a caution, as the woman had not lodged a formal complaint with us. But we held him until we had time to check out what you were telling me. We went to his residence, if you can call the shed in which he's living a residence. He has plenty of equipment -- electrical equipment. My men did a quick initial search and are doing a much more thorough one now. They turned up an odd clue. A flip-flop. One flip-flop, not a size that our Carl could have worn. While that alone is not incriminating in and of itself, it could have been left by any number of people, it was an odd brand with an odd color. The matching flip-flop? Interestingly, young Al from next door had it with him this morning. He said it belonged to the dead lifeguard. Al said he found it on the sidewalk this morning, halfway from here to the beach. He picked it up and was bringing it back to Roger, the dead lifeguard. Apparently, it is a very unique brand and color. Fingerprints on the one found at Carl's indicate that it did belong to Roger, so Roger had been there at Carl's. Last night. Al said to us this morning that he and the girls," Detective Chapman motioned upstairs, indicating Robin and Caela, "were waiting for Roger, then the four of them were to have supper and do the boardwalk last night. Al says Roger never showed up." Detective Chapman waited for a response, but Bill and Ann stood quietly, letting Detective Chapman finish his story and make any conjectures he felt he wanted to.

"So," he continued, "we have a dead woman here, we have a dead man at the beach, whom we can place at this Carl's place at the approximate time of death, and we have descriptions from several witnesses that match that woman upstairs – that Catarina Blackpaw -- who is so anxious to leave."

Bill started to become alarmed. Right at that minute, Catarina was upstairs with the others who were unaware they might be in danger. Bill did not want this to turn into a hostage situation. No telling if this Catarina person was armed. But before he could suggest they move back upstairs, just in case, the detective continued.

"I am glad you called me, filled me in, asked me to stop in to take another look. I think it will be worth taking her down to the station for some questioning. We sure as heck are not releasing Carl yet, not with the evidence, albeit extremely circumstantial, that we have connecting him to the lifeguard's murder and now perhaps of his complicity with this Catarina Blackpaw."

"Yet, as odd a name as it is, Suzanne's husband did have a cousin named that," Ann answered the detective's unasked question.

"Well, if the two of them know each other, and had that argument on the boardwalk earlier today, after two murders, then I feel I should take her in for questioning. Yes, we are pretty sure it was two murders. You say she's the homeowner's cousin?"

"Homeowner's deceased husband's cousin from Maine. But frankly, I am suspicious about that, and should have known before now that she may be an imposter. Sorry, Ann, I thought it was just me, and then Robin just being fanciful. I had the boys back in Buckelsmere run a check on the name Catarina Blackpaw. Still living, still in Maine. I called her this morning but got no answer. I will get you the phone number," Bill said to the detective.

"Robin?" Ann asked.

"Yes, she told John and me earlier in the week that she saw Catarina doing something . . . without her eyepatch on. As if she needed both eyes to do it. I thought it odd at the time, but so much has happened in the meantime, I didn't think of that again until today. And I thought it odd when Suzanne asked Catarina about the house in Buckelsmere and Catarina appeared to know nothing about it. Again, it could have just been a bad memory."

Detective Chapman nodded. "Yes, let's have her to come down here. Let me first call and ask the squad car to pull around quietly for backup." He walked off a few feet and tapped his phone, and directed whomever was on the other end to come. It was only seconds before the patrol car pulled up to the curb. Detective Chapman gave a wave to the driver. Two uniformed officers, a man and a woman got out and came towards them.

"Okay, let's ask this Ms. Blackpaw to come down here and come with me to the station.

Chapter 16

Afternoon, July 6

Ann and Bill went to the Police Station with Detective Chapman, the two officers and Catarina. Not as her advocates or friends, but as police officers. Catarina had done nothing the last four days to encourage their friendship. Detective Chapman had not insisted, but both Ann and Bill could sense the urgency of his request that they accompany him and Catarina to the station for her questioning. Ann knew that the Detective was being cautious and wanted them close at hand, in case the whole case went topsy-turvy as he delved deeper into both Catarina and Carl.

Catarina sat behind the interview desk, eyes flashing, obviously nervous and upset by the turn of events this morning. Ann and Bill hung back against the side wall, trying to sit quietly, motionless, so as to not be a distraction during Detective Chapman's interview. But as it turned out, there wasn't going to be much of an interview.

When Detective Chapman arrived in the interview room, having given Catarina a good fifteen minutes to think about things and the situation, he was carrying a brown paper bag. He walked over to the interview table, upturned the bag, and dumped a pile of tangled jewelry out onto the top of the table.

Catarina stared at it, seemingly unmoved. Ann and Bill peered at it as best they could from their position, careful not to draw attention to themselves. Catarina looked up at Detective Chapman, and waited. The Detective took his time, and finally sat opposite Catarina.

"Do you know what this is?" he asked Catarina.

Catarina looked at the jewelry with her one eye. Ann wondered how soon the detective would reveal all he knew.

Detective Chapman ran his hands over the pile, spreading it out, letting it shimmer and shine in the halogen overhead lighting.

"This," he started, "this pile of jewelry is what we found at Carl Green's residence. Just lying about. Carl didn't even think he ought to hide it away. This jewelry is from the house break-ins and thefts this last few weeks." The detective waited for Catarina to react, but so far nothing from her. Ann watched for a twitch, shortness of breath – something. Detective Chapman continued.

"Do you know anything about this?"

"No," Catarina said quietly.

"Okay, let's try it this way. I'll start telling the facts as we know them and you just jump in anytime you feel like it.

"One. You were having a heated argument with Carl this morning on the boardwalk. You were yelling at him to stay away from you.

"Two. These rings and bracelets here," he said, singling out a few things out of the pile and pushing them slowly across the table directly at Catarina, "these belonged to Marie Ross, the woman who was murdered below the house where you are staying. Carl stole them from her when he murdered her, we believe. Your friend, Carl Green."

Ann noted Catarina had started to clench and unclench her fists in her lap under the desk as she stared at Marie's rings and bracelets.

"Three. Carl is here, too. In the next room. Carl is talking. Boasting, in fact, that you put him up to it, and that he did murder Marie."

"No, I never! I absolutely never –"

"And four. We know the eyepatch is phony. We know you are not really Catarina Blackpaw. So please, knock off the pretense!" He finished.

113

Catarina ripped the eyepatch off, blinking her eyes as the uncovered one became accustomed to the light.

"Now," Detective Chapman continued more quietly, "let's start at the beginning and work through your part in all this. The better you cooperate, the better your chances are in this double murder case."

"Double murder?" Catarina asked, her voice cracking over the words.

"Yes, didn't I mention? Five. When confronted with the evidence we have from his residence, Carl also confessed killing that young lifeguard in the process of covering up the murder of Marie and his jewelry thieving profession. Seems the young lifeguard witnessed his killing Marie, and then he realized at Carl's house later that Carl was also the local thief we've been looking for."

Catarina went white. Ann was sure she'd fall off the chair, but to her credit, Catarina – or whoever she really was – took a deep breath, straightened her back in the chair and proceeded to tell the detective everything.

Detective Chapman walked Ann and Bill out of the station when they had finished with Karen Marks, the fake Catarina's real name. She had told the complete story, her version at least, throwing herself on the mercy of the authorities as she knew she wasn't responsible for the murders and wanted to be sure they knew this.

"I want to thank you two. I am very glad you were here in Ocean City and cared enough to approach me. I know some police departments would not have welcomed the information and suggestions you offered. It made finding the jewelry burglar and solving these two murders relatively simple and quick. I'm not sure we would have linked everything together to one perpetrator, let alone close all three cases within only a couple of days like we have."

Bill wondered how much Ann would share. He left it to her and just nodded agreement as she spoke.

The Diamond Dunes Murders

"Well, Detective, it was just too coincidental about Marie, the hat, her murder, then the second murder. Then of course, Catarina – rather, Karen – we began to realize she could not be the real Catarina as the week went on. She just didn't know things she should have known, and when my daughter saw her take her eyepatch off to look at something, that put us on guard. We were ready to send her on her way today, after exposing her as a fraud, but then there were the two murders. The theft of the jewelry from Marie in broad daylight, post-mortem, that just didn't fit. Breaking and entering to steal jewelry, okay, but not changing his M.O. to murder in broad daylight for a set of wedding rings and a bracelet or two. I knew there was another reason right then for Marie's death. It had to be tied to wearing Suzanne's hat and Marie's returning to Suzanne's house. He was waiting for Suzanne."

Bill cringed. He knew it was true. He knew he didn't understand it, and that worried him. What was going on with Suzanne? How could she be connected to all this?

"Well, all I know is we have the thief with stolen jewelry at his home and he has confessed to that. He boasted about killing Marie when that got out of hand. He says he was pressing her for information about treasure. We'll need to know more about that. And then Carl started boasting about how he killed that young lifeguard to silence him and keep him from going to the police. Carl has a screw loose somewhere. Not careful. Not discreet. Thought he'd go rogue and secure whatever treasure there was without cutting Karen in on her share.

"As for Karen's part in all this, I suspect it will a much lesser charge. Carl's already admitted all Karen wanted was his expertise with the metal detector, and then to approach Suzanne. It turned out he was mistaken and confronted Marie. He used some strong language to persuade her to tell where she had hidden this alleged treasure. And when that didn't work, he used some electrical cord he had handy to scare her. But it apparently Carl went too far with that and Marie ended up dead. I think Karen will get off lightly, unless the real Catarina comes and presses charges over the impersonation part. Carl was bragging that it was all him and that she was a twit. His word, twit. Karen had nothing to do with the jewelry thefts and nothing to do with the murder of the lifeguard. If it hadn't been for you two being under the same roof as her, they might have gotten away with it. They both admitted they were headed away from here today as soon as they could. To disappear and blend in somewhere else, undetected."

"I've known Suzanne for twenty some years. She has never mentioned a treasure or anything that could be misconstrued as treasure. I can't imagine what they were talking about," Ann said.

"Carl said that Karen told him it was something that her father and Suzanne's father-in-law came into possession of during WWII in Europe. Her father had spent the proceeds from the sale of his half, so she looked up Aldo's family online, decided to impersonate Catarina, which was quite a feat, to see if she could find out how much of Suzanne's half was left and then to steal it," Detective Chapman said. He could see the look of disbelief on Ann and Bill's faced. He shook his head.

"I know. Sounds ridiculous. But we have seen it all, as I am sure you have. Greed, stupidity, arrogance. These two are amateurs in the scheme of things. The jewel thefts, then Carl's planting the jewelry in the sand at night to 'find' it the next day with his metal detector – it gave him enough income between fencing it and returning some of it for the reward offered to live okay. But then he thought he'd cash in, as he put it, on this deal with Karen. Well, thanks again, glad to have had your help," Detective Chapman said, but he still wondered how much they knew or had discovered that they were not sharing with him. He admitted to himself that he got that this woman 'Criminal Investigative Consultant' saw connections and was able to piece together the scenario that she and her younger police friend had brought to him earlier in the day. He had been skeptical, but had followed up on it, thank God, solving what appeared to be three separate cases quickly, efficiently and to the back-slapping congratulations from everyone at the station. He told himself that this was a lesson learned – don't write any information off, no matter how kooky it sounded.

Detective Chapman watched the two leave together. He wondered about them, but only for as long as it took for them to walk down the sidewalk and around the next corner out of sight.

In her absence, Suzanne had packed the rest of Karen's things that she had found lying around into Karen's duffle bag. Karen had called someone from jail and they had called Suzanne to explain they were coming around to pick up the bag and post Karen's bail sometime later that afternoon. Suzanne told the person on the phone that the bag, Karen's keys, everything associated with Karen would be out on the front step – take it and don't ever come back.

Then in a fury, Suzanne had closed up the rollaway cot and everything associated with that woman. After she finished that, and in tears by then, Suzanne slammed her way into her bathroom for a long hot soak in her tub.

Robin, Caela and Che-Che spent the time trying hard not to be in the way, not to appear concerned or worried over Suzanne's actions. When Suzanne announced she was going upstairs and take a long hot bath, obviously upset but explaining she just needed some time alone, they had been relieved to let her go and have the space and time she needed to cool off and calm down after the horrible ordeal they had all been through. Che-Che explained to the girls that sometimes a woman just needed a good cry – regardless if it was logical or warranted or not. It had been a very upsetting couple of days, and Suzanne was obviously feeling too much at the center of it, and responsible for it. There was still so much they did not know or understand. When Ann and Bill returned from the police station, maybe they could all sit around together over a revitalizing meal and things would start to look better. Che-Che rose from her spot on the couch and poured a large glass of white wine.

"If all else fails," was all she said and walked out and up the staircase to Suzanne's private area. When she returned to the living area, she noticed Robin and Caela glued to the computer screen.

"What's up?"

"Well, you said 'dinner', so I googled 'stress relieving dinner'. All I find is that we ought to serve spinach, romaine lettuce, swiss chard. Like yuck. I thought I'd call in an order to the corner seafood place for take-out. I can do that, only . . ." Caela said.

"Yes, I know. I'll give you my credit card. My treat. Let's think about this," Che-Che said. Caela beamed with pride. As Che-Che said, it had been a very stressful couple of days. Caela was pleased she had a good idea, affirming her belief that just because she was cute and pert, that wasn't exclusive of also being bright.

"Let's see what it says… hmmm. Fatty fish, greens, whole grains. Let's do this. We'll order some salmon and tuna, kabobs and broiled, some whole wheat pasta in olive oil and cheese with veggies, and a large Caesar salad. That ought to cover those bases you mentioned, Caela," Che-Che suggested.

"I'll pick the tomatoes out," Robin said.

"No worries, easy enough to do," Che-Che said. "Let's call it in, tell them 6:00 p.m. for pickup. If your mom and Bill are not back by then, I'll go with you. It's only two blocks. I could do with the fresh air and the walk actually. Before Suzanne rejoins us, let's get the table set, lemonade and iced tea made, the place picked up. Suzanne will feel good about all that. It will show we care. Okay, let's get to it."

"Um, Che-Che one thing – dessert? Caela asked.

"Ha, right you are! I'll see what they have when we get there and we'll splurge – cheesecake, pie, whatever there is. I'm sure there is still ice cream in the freezer, too. Don't worry, Caela. It'll be a stress relieving feast if there ever was one! Get a candle or two as well if you can. Suzanne likes candles."

The Diamond Dunes Murders

The three got to work getting the living area picked up, the kitchen cleaned, the dining table set for seven instead of eight. Robin took the eighth chair that had been Catarina's chair all week and put it out of sight in her mom's bedroom. Caela found some candle tapers and situated them on the table with a shorebird sculpture she found in the buffet as an arrangement. Robin busied herself making lemonade from a frozen can of concentrate in the freezer and then boiling a large pan of water to make into iced tea with teabags. Suzanne liked her tea with fruit cut and squeezed into it, so Robin searched the refrigerator for oranges, lemons and limes.

It was still all quiet from Suzanne's suite an hour or so later when Ann and Bill arrived home. Che-Che, Robin and Caela watched them come in and drop their keys and things onto the little table in the entryway, trying to gauge their moods and what was to come.

"Where's Suzanne?" Bill asked.

"Upstairs. Hot bath," Che-Che said with a knowingly look at Ann, "She'll have heard you arrive, so she will join us soon, I'm sure. She just needed some alone time, that's all. Caela has taken control of dinner. I'll run over with the girls and pick it up soon. Robin has fresh drinks ready there on the island."

"Wonderful," Ann exclaimed. "You girls have done a terrific, thoughtful job. Look at this place – immaculate and all ready for dinner! It has been a very long, very difficult few days, I know. I know Suzanne will definitely appreciate what you have done as well. We'll go over what happened at the police station after dinner. I'm starving now that I think about it," Ann added, flopping down in cushioned chair.

Chapter 17

That Same Night, July 6

After they had devoured the fish, pasta and salad dinner, the group of friends packed the cardboard take away containers and paper plates into a trash bag to go downstairs to the large trash receptacles. Silverware and glassware were quickly rinsed and loaded into the dishwasher.

Bill cornered Suzanne alone at the sink while the others took their desserts and drinks into the living room.

"Suzanne, I wish I had known," Bill said, keeping his voice low. "I wish I had suspected more than I did. I feel like – "

"Bill, stop. That is not necessary. I should never have let that stranger into my home. I thought, well, who else but the real Catarina Blackpaw would come here and weasel in. When I think of the danger that I ended up putting us all in, putting those girls in!"

"You couldn't have known what would happen. When Marie was killed, when I realized that the murderer meant to pressure you -- that it might have been you. I'm, I'm sorry, I can't seem to say anything intelligent," Bill stuttered. What had happened so suddenly last night, the revelation from Karen and Carl today at the police station had left Bill overanxious about Suzanne. And about the future.

The future, his future, their future.

Suzanne turned and put her hand on his arm, "Bill, it's okay. It turned out okay. Life is too unpredictable to ever know what might happen. It will do no good to worry about it. Lord knows, I've had to learn that lesson the hard way. Yes, I had a few hard moments with all of this, trying to put it all together, trying to understand the why of it, to understand that even here at the shore during a glorious week of sun and beach and friends that there is evil and deception and, and well things can happen so fast and there is no way to stop it happening. No way to change it or go back to before. My God, Bill, how will I ever look the neighbors in the eye again? Marie is dead because of me!"

"No, not because of you. Don't ever think of it that way. Yes, it happened here. Yes, we all were part of the complications associated with this crime, but that man – he was responsible, not you. NOT you, for merely being you. Jesus! I don't know what I would have done if –" Bill said, his voice shaking and increasing in volume, and finally cracking before he realized what he was admitting out loud. He looked up at her face in horror. Had he overstepped, had he blown it all before he'd even given it a descent start?

"Bill, dear Bill," Suzanne softly said, smiling. "I am still here. For some reason, I am still here. Maybe, if I dare say, maybe we know what that reason might be."

Bill drew a rasping breath, holding back the sob he felt might leak out and embarrass him totally. He took her hand in his and held it, sensing its warmth, aware there were too many people in the room adjacent to scoop her up into his arms and kiss her like he would have liked to. It was only with teeth grinding self-control that he refrained. He only held her hand. He choked back any further emotion, nodded his head to her in agreement, and silent acknowledgement of a future, of their unknown future as a couple. It had been declared between them now, no matter how awkwardly.

Ann figured they had had enough time alone at the sink to work out whatever the tension was between them and called out to them. "Hey, you two, bring some more lemonade, and let's discuss a few things we all have on our minds."

Bill let go of Suzanne's hand unwillingly, but in a way glad that Ann's request helped get the evening back to normal. Suzanne grabbed the pitcher and headed to the living room to refill glasses.

Once glasses were topped off, and Bill and Suzanne had taken seats, John started the conversation. "Okay, let's recap because tomorrow we all head home. We know now that this Catarina character was an imposter. Her real name was Karen Marks. That she came to try to get in touch with Suzanne because she believed there was some kind of treasure that her father and Aldo Beck had acquired back in the 1940's."

Ann picked up the story. "Karen, the imposter, must have believed this story she had grown up hearing. That her father and Aldo Beck were G.I.'s together in Austria at the end of the war. They made friends with a woman who plotted with the two of them to get her out of Austria and on her way to England and then America in exchange for a bag of jewels she claimed she had stolen from the Austrian royal family at the end of the first World War as they escaped into Switzerland in 1919. She was a maid and was responsible for many of the royal family's personal things including some jewels. When they all got on the train to Switzerland, she quietly ducked out and disappeared into the countryside waiting her chance to escape. By the time the royal family realized what had happened, she was hundreds of miles away and there was no way to trace her. Twenty-five years of hiding out, keeping her treasure safe from bandits and then the Nazi's – she just wanted out – to come to America to spend the rest of her life. Karen alleges that the woman traded the treasure she still had to Aldo and her dad for anonymous and safe passage across the Atlantic.

"So, we have two G.I.'s with a sack of jewels that they divided between themselves after getting the woman on her way to England first, then America afterwards, never to see her again. Karen says her father had spent, squandered more likely, his half of the treasure, had lived high for years before it ran out. He has since passed away, as has Aldo, but he gave Karen Aldo's name. She claimed in today's interview that she merely googled Aldo Beck, found out he had died, that his son had died, but you were still alive and owned this property in Ocean City. She swore she didn't know about the Buckelsmere house, that her internet search turned up this house, and she never thought to keep looking for other property. She then looked up Frank's family, distant family, and by hook and by crook, learned he had a cousin in Maine he had visited as a child. So, she went to where the real Catarina Blackpaw lives, found out what she could, hence the fake eye-patch, and came here knowing Suzanne would have very little knowledge of the real Catarina but if she did check up on her, Catarina was a real person and a real cousin of Frank's."

Che-Che said, "We should have seen all the little clues, the fake eye-patch, the -- "

"The sand I found on the floors and furniture from their using that metal detector in here," Suzanne added.

"That she didn't know about the house in Buckelsmere where Aldo and Frank lived most of their lives. I should have really caught that one."

"The hair color was fake, newly done. It was one reason she was afraid to go into the ocean."

"Her complete insistence on getting in here and staying. Who does that?"

"And, well, I am not so sure, Suzanne," Robin interrupted. She shot her mom, John and Bill a quick glance, knowing she should have shared this earlier. "Karen was sneaking around one day. Looking at things, looking through things. It makes sense now knowing she was looking for some kind of treasure. She was especially interested in that little table," Robin said pointing at the table across the room.

"The little oak sewing stand?" Suzanne asked. "I brought that down from home as I needed something small to put in that spot. It was Frank's favorite piece at home. I liked having it here as a memory of him."

"Yes, she took everything out of it, emptied it as she did other things in here, but this time she took a cell phone photo of the inside of the drawer itself." Robin stopped. There was a silence as everyone digested this.

Suzanne stood and went to the little sewing table that had three small drawers, originally for thread and sewing equipment back when most sewing was still done by hand.

"Which drawer?"

"I don't really remember. I was more or less hiding over there in the doorway. I didn't want her to see me."

Suzanne took the top drawer out and over to the kitchen island where she emptied it onto the granite countertop. Everyone else had risen and joined her there. They all took a good look at the little drawer. Nothing. Nothing unusual. Suzanne loaded it back up again and took it back to the table reinserting it. Then she pulled out the middle drawer and brought it to the kitchen island, emptied it, but with the same result. But when the third drawer was emptied out and examined, they found some written symbols on the bottom. They all took a long hard look at it and tried to decide why this would have been of interest to Catarina.

On the inside bottom of the little oak drawer, were hand written symbols in heavy black ink, almost as if the writer wanted to be sure they didn't fade or wipe off.

Each person took a turn holding the little drawer and studying the symbols. No one had a good explanation.

"Yep, that's it, that is what Karen took photos of, so it must mean something."

Suzanne's stomach did a couple of flips. She had seen marks like this before, but she quickly decided to keep that revelation to herself. She'd been taken in by this Catarina imposter and although she'd stake her life on the true and good nature of everyone in the room, she knew she better just keep this to herself, for now at least.

At home in Buckelsmere, at the house that had been Aldo's, and then Frank's and hers, there was a safe with the normal things in it – deeds, investments, her will, her jewelry when she traveled. She'd taken to backing up her computer and putting the backed-up files in there on DVD's and on thumb drives as well. When Frank died, and she'd had to deal with that and with the estate, she'd found a ledger of dates and numbers with many lines of symbols similar to these. She was sure of it. At the time, she'd had no idea what it was. The dates were mostly from Aldo's lifetime, and in his handwriting, now that she thought about it. Then when Aldo had passed away, the entries had changed to Frank's handwriting for the last few entries. That's why she had kept it – out of sentimentality. And now she suspected that it probably was significant.

"Suzanne?" John asked, bringing her attention back to the present.

"Oh, I'm sorry, my mind was drifting," Suzanne said. "What were you asking?"

"Was Frank or his dad a Freemason?" John repeated.

"Freemason?" Suzanne answered, thinking the change of topics rather abrupt and odd.

"These symbols, I've seen them before. They are part of what's called the Freemason's Cipher. I do ciphers, cryptograms, crosswords, word jumbles – you know. My mind works like that," John explained.

"Well, good then. Tell us what they mean," Suzanne said, avoiding answering John's question.

John studied the symbols carefully. He took a piece of paper and copied them onto it, so Suzanne could fill the drawer back up and replace it in the table.

"Okay, Frank's dad or maybe Frank himself, wrote these symbols here onto the drawer so there would be some kind of a permanent record of these symbols. It would be too easy for a slip of paper to be mislaid or destroyed."

Suzanne was recalling what Frank's last words to her were as he boarded the plane for Iraq, "Throw nothing out. Nothing, until I get back." It seemed so odd to her at the time, now she was beginning to piece things together in her mind, in her memory as images struggled to the surface of her consciousness.

"Let me show you all how this cipher works. One first draws the grids like this," John said, drawing four grids onto the paper below the symbols he had copied from the bottom of the drawer.

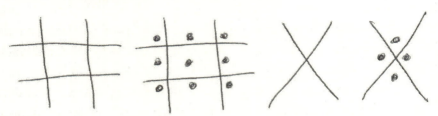

"Next we take the alphabet and fit it into the slots.

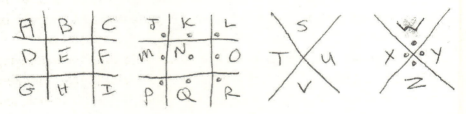

"Then you take the shapes we have from the drawer and match them up, giving us corresponding letters. This is called a direct cipher, with no mixing up of the letters to make it more difficult. Let's see what, if anything, we get," John said and then worked carefully, shape by shape writing each matching letter underneath the shape.

The Diamond Dunes Murders

With this ring. Suzanne knew. She knew instantly what that meant, but decided again not to share it. She'd check it out first alone when she returned home to Buckelsmere. The answer lay there – at home in Buckelsmere.

"Jeepers!" Caela was the first to speak, breaking the others' personal thoughts. She looked over John's shoulder, reading what he had written, "Another mystery!"

"Yes, well, I suspect it may a clue to the 'key' word that we would need for the additional cipher. If there *is* another cipher. Let me explain. If a word is placed at the beginning of the rest of the alphabet being put into the grids, then it is very hard for anyone to crack the cipher. That word, or series of letters (because it does not have to be a word per se), would be known to only one or a few people. Without that key word, there is no way we will ever decode what this all means. The simple initial code 'With this ring' is a clue for remembering whatever the cipher maker used as the beginning of the real sequence of letters in their cipher. It could be anything."

John was aware Suzanne had not said anything. He knew he better wrap this up and end it now. There would be no treasure hunt tonight, not here in this shore house. John took the piece of paper, folded it in half and handed it to Suzanne. She took it without looking at him in the eyes, walked over to the little table and put it into the drawer that had the cipher on the bottom. She swallowed, drew a steadying breath, and found her voice.

"Guess we'll never know. At least not tonight. I feel a chill. I think the weather is turning again. Che-Che, be a dear and make me some hot tea while I fetch a sweater, anyone else?"

"I'd be glad to. I'm feeling like a bracer myself. That last bit about treasures and ciphers has kind of overwhelmed me. I don't know what I was expecting, but for a few minutes, it was like we were in a movie. Hidden treasure, ciphers, odd characters, murd—"

y it," Ann interrupted. "Let's not talk about that night. We ...ely tired, we're all wrung out from the police investigation, and the revelation of what was happening right here under our noses. Let's try to think on pleasant things, and I think, for one, I need to get to bed," Ann informed them. Not only did she know that Robin and Caela had better get to bed as they would lay awake and hash this one over for hours once in bed with the lights out, but she could see Suzanne was terribly distressed. She needed more than a soothing cup of tea.

"Che-Che, let me help. You two girls head on up to bed. Morning will be here too soon. We'll be packing, cleaning up and heading home at lunchtime. I promised Caela's mom I'd have her home midafternoon, before dinner at the latest," Ann directed. As she went into the kitchen, she grabbed the bourbon bottle off the end of the counter, opened the refrigerator and grabbed a lemon, and then a box of mint tea bags out of the cupboard.

"Good idea," Che-Che said, when she saw where this was going. "Make us all a good stiff one," Che-Che suggested. When the water was at a boil, Ann poured it over the mint tea bags in four mugs, then squeezed a quarter of the lemon into each mug, stirred in a large spoonful of brown sugar and finally a generous jigger of bourbon. She handed them around to the others, Suzanne having returned with a warm sweater against the chill she was feeling.

"Bottoms up." Ann watched Suzanne drink hers slowly. Her color did come back eventually, the bourbon and tea warming and soothing. But Ann could feel an icy cold radiating from Suzanne. Suzanne was holding something back from them, something very important. Ann knew the secret Suzanne kept was hers alone. They all had secrets, Ann would not deny that. Sometimes it was best not to press to know those secrets. The complications that revealing the secrets caused often was not worth knowing. Ann thought back to Scotland, and back to a country inn just a few years ago. Secrets that she herself held very close and very private. No one knew. No one would ever know

Chapter 18

Morning, July 7

Ann hadn't slept much, even with the benefit of the hot toddy. When everyone else had turned in, she did the same, but the feeling of uneasiness edged closer and closer, and sleep eluded her.

Too much had happened this week. Two much had intruded into their happy little party. But she knew she'd have to face each little problem as it presented itself for resolution. She'd deal with each one, and hopefully either diffuse it, or improve it, or be able to forget about it.

Ann must have drifted off to sleep at some point because she awoke in the gray of predawn, as the birds were beginning to chirp. No doubt just house sparrows, but chirping they were. She moved slowly to see the time on the alarm clock without disturbing John. 4:45 a.m. Way too early.

Ann had been exhausted before they came on this week's trip to the shore. The broken hip, the change of job and the new home routine. Ann had promised herself a quiet, uneventful week of sun, the sea, and good food and better friends. She had not planned on murder, deception, secrets, the obvious budding romance of Bill and Suzanne, and of course Robin. She was going to have to talk with Robin.

Ann heard noise from the bedroom above theirs. Someone was up. She heard the door open softly and footsteps that eventually diminished and faded away. She rose, slipped off her nightgown and pulled on shorts and a tee-shirt, and headed upstairs. When she got to the 2nd floor landing, all was quiet and no lights were on. All she could hear was the quiet sounds of people sleeping and the breeze against the windows. A sea-breeze. It would be a deliciously nice day. But they were headed home. Home to the real world. So, decision time. Ann knew Robin had not gone downstairs, so she must be upstairs on the roof deck. No time like the present, Ann decided.

Ann turned and continued up the staircase to the roof deck, opening the door and stepping out over the dew damp decking in the gray predawn light. Robin sat in a chair, looking east to the sea, awaiting the sunrise. Ann walked over to her and sat alongside in a second chair

"Awfully early to be up."

"Couldn't sleep. Too much chasing around in my head," Robin said.

"I know, me too. I don't know how anyone slept the last two nights. When I get home, I might sleep for a week."

Robin gave a light, short laugh.

"Mom, I've been thinking about a lot of things," Robin started.

Oh no, too soon. Here it comes, Ann thought. Be calm, be brave, be thoughtful, be truthful, but most of all, be calm, Ann told herself.

Robin continued, "I overheard you, Suzanne and Che-Che talking about how I am adopted. About never being part of the D.A.R."

"Yes, well, that is true. You are adopted, you know that. But since day one, you have been my daughter. And eventually John's daughter."

"I know that. I just am not sure how I feel about knowing that out there somewhere – I don't even know where -- there are people who are my biological mother and father. Perfect strangers. People who might be wonderful people or horrible people – like Karen and Carl!"

Ann didn't interrupt Robin. Better for Robin to get it all out, all her thoughts, fears and questions. Ann sat as quietly as she could, without moving, trying to make no sound. Robin took a deep breath and continued.

"I've been thinking about all that, in the middle of all the drama of this week. I'm a little confused and curious, but I have been afraid to bring it up."

"Never be afraid to ask me anything. If I can, I will answer you."

"I know, I've known that all along. I just maybe think I am afraid to know. Maybe not knowing would be better."

"How about this, then. I will share a little now. And as you get older and it becomes more important to you that you know other parts of the story, I will share them with you then. You can feel free to ask at any time, and I will tell you what I know. How about that? That way you can know, but not have to know so much today that it is overwhelming?"

Robin sat silently, watching the eastern horizon for the sun to lift above the horizon.

"Okay, tell me about family first."

"It takes two to be a family, only two. So, for years it was just you and me – we were family. Everyone thought of us as a family, *we* thought of us as family. No one walked around looking for blood tests and birth certificates. Then John came into our lives eight years ago and now there are three in our family. All it took for him to be family was to say a few words and sign a paper. Keep that in mind. That's all it took to be part of our family in the eyes of the law, in the eyes of the rest of our family and in the eyes of all our friends."

"I didn't think about that. That he's not 'blood' either. He's part of our family, but not blood related."

"No, but he is family. That's how we look at you as our daughter. Yes, our daughter. Maybe not blood, but no different. Think of all the people in the world. There are many thinking their dad is their dad, when he's not, really. You are old enough to understand that happens from time to time. 'Families' are the people that live together, that declare themselves to be family. No papers, no medical tests. Just a decision to be 'family.' "

"I like that. A decision to be a family. I like that. But . . . "

"Yes, the 'who?' question. This is what I can tell you now. When you get older it may be appropriate to tell you more. Some of the story isn't mine to tell. I know that sounds evasive, but I made promises a long time ago, and I will honor those promises."

"For secrecy?"

"More like discretion and timeliness."

"I see. Like a movie rating -- PG, R, etc."

"Yes, good analogy. Time and age appropriate revelations. Your biological mother died. She became ill at a young age and passed away. Your father was not in a position to take you or your mother when you were born. He asked me, through a dear mutual acquaintance, if I would take you and raise you as my own. I owed this man a great deal. So, I said yes. I could not have said otherwise once you were placed in my arms that day. You were mine, all mine." The memory of that day, those first moments with infant Robin flooded back over Ann as she remembered Robin's tiny fingers and delicate eyelashes, the blush on her baby cheeks – so rosy. "I called you Robin. And here we are."

"Do you think my real dad wonders about me?"

"Yes, I'm sure he does. I believe he gets reports about you. Not from me, I felt I must stay away. He's a man of extreme power and importance. Yet, he keeps a watchful and thankfully very benevolent eye on you from afar."

"Will I ever know who he is, or meet him?"

"That, sweetie, I don't know. Let's just go along for a while, with you knowing this much and see what develops. I knew one day you'd ask, but I have to admit it came sooner than I expected. And with all that's happened this week . . ."

"Look – there's the sun! The sun's rising!" Robin exclaimed. Ann smiled. And just that fast, the conversation was over, and the new day dawned.

Together in smiling silence they watched the sun step up over the horizon and become full and bright in the cloudless blue infinity. Ann realized the buzzing in her head, the distant voice calling to her from across the sea had ceased. All would be well now for a while.

"Come on, let's get something to eat."

"Okay," Robin agreed. They headed downstairs together.

The Diamond Dunes Murders

After a few hours of putting sheets and towels into the washer and dryer and then remaking the beds, running the vacuum around and doing some general picking up as they collected their personal things and packed their bags, they each took their suitcase down to the car for the drive home.

Caela ducked away out of sight to speak with Al, who was waiting for her on his front porch. They agreed they'd email each other, text and talk on their cellphones when possible. Al updated them on how his family had calmed down, his sister Kathy and husband and little Jack had gone back to Philadelphia already with Rob to make final arrangements for Marie's funeral. His mom and dad would attend that, but he figured he'd escape it by being too distant a relative. He'd have to go to Roger's service, but the whole lifeguard group would go to the calling hours together, so he wasn't dreading it too badly. He was still having nightmares about seagulls and all, but had been told they would eventually stop. He sure hoped so.

Caela mentioned her private high school's Homecoming Weekend that coincided with the village's Scavenger Hunt in early October. Maybe he could come up from college for that, it would be so awesome if he could. Al agreed it would be, but he'd have to see how his first semester at college was going at that point.

When Che-Che had her bag and laptop in her car, she hollered to Ann and Suzanne, "We need a trip to Louisiana. I'm stuck on an ancestor and need to go down there for a bit of hands-on research. Let's pick a date." Then off she went, convertible top down, her hair held in a kerchief like movie stars of old, heading back to quiet Mr. Reyes and her life in Pennsylvania.

Bill knew his moment was at hand, while John directed the packing of the suitcases, cooler and leftover supplies into the back of his Jeep. Bill took Suzanne's arm and pulled her aside. "Suzanne, the other day, before all the nonsense started, I bought these for you, to replace the one you lost in the sand," he said and handed her the little bag with the Cape May Diamond earrings in it. "They aren't expensive, just something you can wear and not worry if you lose them. And something to remember – well, hopefully only the fun and good parts of this week." Bill pressed the little bag into her hand. She opened it and withdrew the earrings, surprised he had done such a thing, had thought of her like that – someone to buy jewelry for.

"Thank you, Bill, that's a sweet thing to do. I will wear them with pleasure. And I will remember the part of that day we had in Cape May before the phone call from Robin. Thank you," she said and kissed him on the cheek, thought better of it, and then kissed him lightly on his lips. She thought he blushed slightly. "I'll call you. After I get all this Diamond Dunes – Karen stuff straightened out, as soon as the police are done with me and the house," she said eyeing the yellow Police Line – Do Not Cross tape still draped over half of the parking area. Bill nodded. He knew she needed some time. It was harder for a civilian, a non-police person, to come to grips with the things that they had experienced and seen this week. When it was truly over, she'd need some time to digest it, and then she'd be more willing to talk about it. He hoped she'd share with him whatever it was that he sensed she was holding back from them and the police.

Then Bill asked her if he could leave his postcards in her mailbox for mailing. She took them from him and assured him they would be collected later that day, but that he'd be home days before anyone received them. Bill explained when they were received wasn't important. He enjoyed sending them, and he knew his family enjoyed his sharing his adventures.

Ann had watched all this, but tried to not get caught. Seemed too personal in a way. Suzanne was trying hard to appear in control and give them all the impression that everything was okay – they could all leave and go home without a second thought, but Ann knew her too well. Beneath that styled hair, and the designer sportswear, Suzanne was not feeling okay. Ann stepped over to her as Bill took his leave and went to the Jeep to get into the front with John.

"Suzanne," Ann started.

The Diamond Dunes Murders

"No, Ann, it's okay, really. Really. I'm fine. I think I just need some sleep and some quiet for a while to process all this," She laughed, but it came out more of a choke. Ann patted her back.

"You know we are all here for you. If you want one of us to stay and help, just to keep you company, even," Ann suggested.

Suzanne was grateful, but someone staying would only mess up her plans. She smiled, "No, it's okay. I'm going to deal with all this, then come up home for a few days, just to get a change of scenery and attitude. Then when I come back here, it will be my shore house again. Everything that happened this week will be gone, and hopefully soon forgotten. I will give you a call in three or four days."

"Well," Ann smiled a knowing smile and a glance towards where Bill was getting into the passenger side of the front seat of the jeep, "maybe not everything."

Suzanne smiled back at her, conspiratorially. "Yes, not everything. But we'll see. We'll see how that goes; way too early to tell."

Ann nodded, turned, and headed to the Jeep to climb into the back seat. She felt good about helping solve the two murders, even if it was without renumeration this time; anything to help out Suzanne and her neighbors. Ann was feeling very good about her conversation with Robin earlier that morning. There was still plenty to explain eventually, not but today.

Suzanne waved as they pulled out of the car park area under Diamond Dunes. Standing in the sun watching her friends leave and head back to their normal lives. She flicked the postcards in her left hand against her other fingertips. She'd drop them in her mailbox for Bill, and take her new earrings upstairs. Maybe she'd even put them on now! Why not?

She had come up with a plan during the endless sleepless hours the previous night. Her bag was already packed and setting in her room, out of sight. She'd take out the trash so it would not miss collection the next day. She'd call Detective Chapman and say she was going home and ask if she could she take down the police tape if they were finished with Diamond Dunes. Then she'd close up the house for now, pop her suitcase in her car and drive back to her home in Buckelsmere without anyone else knowing. It was there, at her home in Buckelsmere in that little Victorian house, that the secrets and hopefully some answers lay now. Not here at the beach. Like fake Catarina, she'd taken a cell phone photo of the marks on the little drawer. She'd need that and the paper John had written on once she was home. Because after all that happened, what she had learned being married to Frank those few years, and what John had been able to share with the group last night about secrets and ciphers, she knew in her heart that indeed there must be treasure.

The Diamond Dunes Murders

Dear Mom,

I bought you some salt water taffy. The beach was wonderful. I ended up having to help the locals with a situation. I even bought myself a hoodie with "Ocean City, NJ' written on it for the chilly evenings on the boardwalk. Hope to see you soon. I might be bringing a new friend home to visit soon.

Bill

Chapter 19

Night, Buckelsmere, July 7

It was almost dinnertime by the time Suzanne pulled up in the driveway next to her home in Buckelsmere, but she was not hungry. She'd open a can of soup or heat up a frozen pizza later she supposed.

She inserted her key in the lock of the old door and opened it up into her small entryway. The house had been closed up for a couple of weeks now and smelled musty. Setting her suitcase down, she went around and raised all the windows. Luckily it wasn't so warm outside that she'd be letting in the heat. She could tell that by bedtime, the musty smell would be gone.

Suzanne could not get out of her head what Karen told the police was her motivation for asking Carl to help her search and to press her, for information she would not have been able to give. She shuddered. It should have, would have been her dead if only she had not shared her hat with Marie that day. Poor Marie!

All that talk about the Austrian Hungarian royal family and the portion of the crown jewels that supposedly ended up in Aldo's hands. She realized that it could all be bunk. Karen's father could have just been making up the entire story so he could boast in front of his family. Suzanne did not doubt that Karen's father knew Aldo. Why make that up? Aldo had been forthcoming about his service in WWII, ending up in Austria at the end of the war with the U.S. 3rd Army under General Mack Clark. That much seemed too coincidental to be shrugged off.

The Diamond Dunes Murders

Suzanne decided that Karen might someday appear on this very doorstep, her courage and intentions renewed, and with much better thought out plans, and demanding the treasure. Suzanne would have to come up with a plan for that, a solution to it happening at all. Perhaps she would ask Bill, he'd know what she could do legally to stop that from happening.

Flipping the lights on in the dining room, she set her laptop on the table. She didn't have a room dedicated to being just an office, as downstairs she had the entryway, a dining room, living room or parlor as it would have been called back when the house was built in the 1880's, an adequate but older kitchen and the small powder room that she and Frank had fashioned out of the old pantry after Aldo passed away and they had moved in. Upstairs there was a hall bath and three small but adequate bedrooms. She had considered turning a bedroom into an office, but Frank's stern 'Get rid of nothing!' plea when he was leaving had never left her; she had changed nothing in the house since then.

So, she used the dining room table as a desk when she did any paperwork or paid bills. She had her printer on a small filing cabinet in the corner. She shook herself out of her self-pity reverie and focused on the task at hand. She wanted to tackle this by herself. As she had done most everything in the last fifteen years.

Pulling out her cell phone, she found the photo of the cipher at the shore and sent it to the printer via WIFI. When it had printed, she took the page to the table. She would organize everything she knew and then try to figure out the rest.

Frank's parting words to her when he had had to leave for Iraq so suddenly had been "Sell nothing, get rid of nothing. The answer is in the safe. Remember Forever!"

But as a result of following what quite tragically turned out to be Frank's last wishes, Suzanne had kept everything the same since then, almost afraid to break her promise to Frank as he rushed out the door to catch the plane. She *had* changed nothing and as a result had started to feel stuck. Stuck in this house, stuck with an empty life. Stuck. Out of her love and loyalty to Frank, she had never shared these thoughts, not even with Ann. At first, changing anything was the last thing she wanted – she just wanted Frank back. Everything that was there only comforted her for a while, but now, she did want to make changes. How was she to move on, maybe have this new romance with Bill Dancer if she were obsessed with protecting the past so completely?

Suzanne made a bold promise to herself. If in this search she was undertaking she found nothing, if in trying to decode the cipher she was unsuccessful, if after one last consultation with the family lawyer and accountant that there was nothing left to discover about the Beck family or alleged fortune, then she would just call it a day and move on. She'd get rid of things that didn't suit her and at least explore the possibility of this relationship she felt that Bill Dancer was offering her. She'd worry about all that in the next few days. The weight of years of stagnation began to lift, and there was a lightness in her heart, long forgotten, but surprisingly easy to reclaim.

Suzanne wrote down what she knew in a list:

Cipher in drawer 'With This Ring'

It was the Freemason's Cipher but there are variations.

The word 'Forever' must be significant, as it is engraved inside her and Frank's wedding rings. 'Forever' – the last word he said before he left.

The ledger in the safe, and a multipage document along with it, bore the same symbols on them.

Frank's sense of urgency that she get rid of nothing implied that something important might be lost if she did – a clue, a key or the actual treasure

Aldo's war stories did parallel those told by Karen.

Suzanne flipped the laptop open and waited until the screen came to life. She typed in "Freemason Cipher" on the google search bar. Lots of sites were listed. After reading three or four, which all basically said the

The Diamond Dunes Murders

same thing, and after she had also looked up everything John had said the night before, she learned that the Freemason's Cipher was invented by the Mason's in the 1700's so they could keep their history, records and rites private, and the cipher could be used between the lodge members for communication.

To answer John's question, yes, both Frank and Aldo had been Masons. She felt funny holding that fact back last night, but she was giving out no information to anyone until she could understand what was going on. So, Aldo and Frank very well might have been very familiar with this cipher.

Suzanne took a blank sheet of paper and, like John, drew the grids, the pigpens as some called them, across the page.

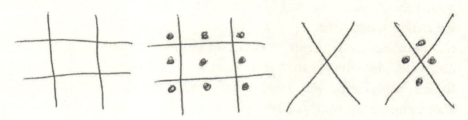

But John had insisted that the first cipher had been easy because it needed to give the clue for the second one. He called it a straight substitution cipher. He had explained by jumbling the letters, it would make it near impossible to decode. She sat and twirled the pencil, trying to think, and finally deciding on the obvious answer, the one Frank had made her promise not to forget – 'Forever'. Suzanne penciled the word into the grid, careful not to duplicate any letters, then filled in the rest of the blanks with the remaining alphabet.

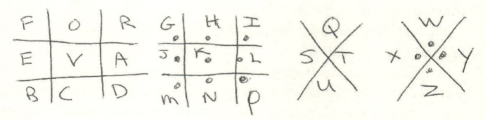

It was there staring at her in the face. Forever. F-O-R-E-V. Convinced she had the grids ready for the next cipher, she got up and went to the coat closet in the hallway. There Aldo had installed an old fashioned safe in the closet on a shelf at eye level. She knew the combination to this safe, it had never been a secret. She and Frank had used it for years, although until Frank had died, she'd no reason for going into it except to place her jewelry there for safe keeping against burglary or fire during their occasional trips and vacations. She lightly turned the dial, listening to the click-click-click as it turned. 6 – 15 – 82, Their wedding date. Then pulled up on the lever handle to expose the inside, about 15" wide by 10" deep and 10" high. Very spacious for what she kept in it – her jewelry, passport, tax returns, deeds, that sort of thing. She gathered it all up and took it to the dining room table.

Spreading it all out on the table, she passed over anything that she had originated, like the tax folders and her own jewelry. She set all that aside to be returned to the safe later. What was left was an old ledger book and a two-page document stuffed inside of it. She had seen all this when she cleaned out the safe after Frank died, needing to find Frank's will and the cemetery plot deed. She had not known what it was, but it was odd enough to keep as a memento rather than throw it out as useless. And last night she remembered instantly upon seeing the cipher in the drawer, that this ledger and paper were full of the same symbols She hoped that she had hidden her surprise and recognition well enough last night. It had been a shock at the very first moment, but then developed into a sense of hope. She hoped she'd now understand what this ledger and paper meant.

Taking another sheet of paper to write on, she started at the beginning where there were symbols after columns of numbers. Working slowly, symbol by symbol, she decoded the headings across the ledger left to right. 'Shape', 'Weight', 'Quantity', 'Sold', 'Value', 'Date'. The numbers in each column meant nothing to her really. The dates started in 1946 after Aldo would have returned home from the war and about when he started his restaurant. Some kind of an inventory on the first few pages. As she studied it, it appeared to be a large inventory of pieces that had not yet been sold. There was no date or value listed next to many of the items in the inventory.

After 1989, the handwriting changed to Frank's, after they had married, and Aldo had passed away. There were only a few entries and updates. Whatever was going on had been kept a secret. Perhaps this was lodge business and wasn't anything to do with anything in her life. The last entry was shortly before Frank had taken out the rather large insurance policy on himself. Whatever it was that he had sold – the dollar value struck her as very similar to what he had paid for that life insurance policy. That life insurance had carried her financially these last fifteen years since he'd been gone. She had never questioned that he had bought life insurance, never really given it much thought about how he had paid for it. Until now when she saw the date and dollar figures in his handwriting made just weeks before he went to Iraq and never came back. He had sold something to buy the insurance that had supported Suzanne.

Suzanne went carefully page by page, but there were no other symbols to use the cipher on. She set the ledger aside. With a slight sense of foreboding, he opened the folded pages of solid symbols. This would no doubt take her a while to decode. Carefully she worked through it character by character. When she finished decoding it, she looked at the page of letters. She then took a pencil and started drawing diagonal lines between what she knew were words. By the time she got to the closing, Suzanne was crying.

> My dearest,
> If you are reading this, I am gone. I am sorry. Sorry for all we will not share together in the years to come. You have discovered the cipher and you have decoded this, and no doubt the inventory as well.
> There is another safe in the basement, behind the wine rack. There is a latch that lets you swing the wine

rack out to reveal the safe. Be careful not to jostle the bottle of champagne from our wedding. Once you see it, you will know what to do. This is the only place you will have to look. Whatever you find, whatever is left at this point, take it, use it wisely and move on.

 Live long and live happy, my love.

 Forever, Frank.

 Suzanne wept for Frank, gone. She wept for herself, alone. She wept for having not known, not figured out there even *was* something to figure out. She wept in exhaustion. When she was calm again, she got up to find a flashlight. She stopped at the kitchen sink to wet a towel and wipe her face clean and then dry.

 The basement steps, old, wooden and narrow, went from a doorway in the kitchen and dropped down into the dark basement. It was the original basement, never redone. Frank had poo-poo'd the idea of finishing it. He always said that once he carved out an area for the washer and dryer, furnace, hot water heater and storage, there'd was practically no room left. What did the two of them need with more room anyways?

 As Suzanne walked along, she pulled the strings to turn on single naked bulb lights as she made her way towards the back of the basement where Aldo had installed a floor to ceiling wine rack. It was at least 4 feet wide, now pretty much empty, as Suzanne over the fifteen years had drunk the wine bottle by bottle and not replaced it. Now she just kept the wine she bought up in the kitchen in the refrigerator or on the counter.

 She looked for the bottle of champagne left from their wedding day so many years ago. She had wryly joked that when it was their 50-year anniversary, she'd auction it off and take a world cruise with the proceeds! She lifted the bottle out of its space, and set it onto the top of the washer nearby. Using the flashlight, she peered into that spot, and yes indeed, there did appear to be some kind of a mechanism there. She reached her hand in and pressed on it. Nothing. Okay, she thought, now what? She pulled on it and it separated from the metal portion on the wall, freeing the actual wine rack panel so she could swing it out towards her like a door. Slowly, so as to not endanger any of the bottles still on it, she let the wall wine rack swing out into the room leaving a dark open area in front of her. And yes, there it was – another safe, hung at eye level, with space for more cases of wine below it.

Now what, she thought? With the flashlight she illuminated the safe's dial. She tried the same combination as the safe upstairs used, but it didn't work. She went through all the obvious three number combinations – their anniversary, her birthday, his birthday, their address. She paused, thinking, but trying to not overthink. She remembered what his letter said: be careful with the bottle of wedding champagne, 'once you see it, you'll know.'

Suzanne walked the few steps back out into the light of the basement to the washing machine and picked up the bottle. She looked at the familiar label. God, it seemed like only yesterday they were having those pre-wedding quarrels, good natured but boundary defining, over which champagne to buy, what they ought to print on the label. She smiled, so like him to be so opinionated about the little things. She had won in the end. The label would have their names, the wedding date, and artwork of the flowers that would match her wedding bouquet. And Frank was right, she did know what to do. She studied the label, and there on the label, he had taken a pen and made an editor's notation on the date to reverse the last two numbers. So, instead of reading the wedding date as 6-15-82, he wanted her to read it as 6-15-28. At least that is what she hoped he meant.

She returned to the safe and whisked the dial three times around to clear any previous attempts. Carefully, flashlight in her left hand shining on the dial, she turned it to 6 to the right, 15 to the left and then 28 to the right. Her heart gave a flip when she heard the click of success. She pulled up on the lever handle and peered into the safe with expectant eyes.

The safe was similar to the one upstairs. Aldo must have installed them when he moved to this house in the 1950's. Instead of tax files and ledgers, this safe held soft fabric bags and leather boxes. Too difficult to mess with all this down here in the basement in the bad light and no place to spread things out, Suzanne gathered it up in her arms leaving the flashlight. She spotted an empty plastic laundry basket. Perfect, she thought. She let the things in her arms dropped gently into the basket and then went back to the safe for anything she had left. Once it was all in the laundry basket, and Suzanne was sure she had completely emptied the safe, she turned off the flashlight, leaving it on the washer to use later and headed upstairs, not bothering to try to turn off the overhead lights as she went. She'd come back down later to do that.

Suzanne set the basket, quite heavy for the amount that was in it, on the dining room table and carefully started to unwrap things.

She started with a velvet pouch with an ornate drawstring. She gasped as she pulled out a diamond and sapphire studded tiara. Fit for a princess. At once, she realized that Karen's story must have been true – there had been a treasure after all! It made her breath come short and in gulps. She made herself take several long breaths and count to five to steady herself. After all that had happened this week, she had not expected anything like this.

In the end, she counted two sandwich size velvet bags of loose diamonds and colored stones, the tiara, six leather bags of 4 ducat Franz Joseph gold coins, no doubt they were what was so heavy in the laundry basket, several small boxes of rings and bracelets, all quite gaudy and fragile. She had saved the wooden box for last. It had a tiny golden clasp. When she had pried it open, careful not to break it, the box revealed a clear stone, light yellow-green in color. In the light of the chandelier over the dining room table, it appeared more yellow than green. It was faceted, a bit of an irregular shape, but spectacular as she held it in the palm of her hand and let it sparkle in the light. The size of a flat egg, brilliant in the light, mesmerizing.

Suzanne knew exactly what this stone was, as she had seen it earlier on the internet when she did the quick search on Aldo in the war in Austria, and on what few facts she had learned that Karen had been blurting out at the police station.

They called this the Florentine Diamond, all 137 carats of it sitting in her palm, The Austrian Yellow Diamond, lost at the end of WWI. Most felt it had been sold off and cut into smaller stones. But no. Here it was, she was holding it. As had Charles the Bold in 1476, Pope Julian II, Ferdinand II de' Medici, the Grand Duke of Tuscany, until eventually passing to the Hapsburgs when Francis III Stephen of Lorraine married Empress Maria Theresa of Austria. Suzanne had read about it online; seen photos of it from the early 20th Century. It was worth about $12,000,000 in today's money. The magnitude of the secret Frank and his father before him had kept all those years left her breathless and lightheaded. Perhaps the treasure had, after all, warranted the level of secrecy and protection behind which Frank and Aldo had concealed it. Suzanne suspected neither Aldo nor Frank had fully realized both the monetary and historic value of what they had kept secret and hidden for nearly sixty-five years.

It had grown completely dark outside in the hours Suzanne had been busy with the cipher and sorting the treasure. Suzanne sat at the table with her treasure, just thinking about it all. All it had seen, the horrors it had experienced. It was now clear to her why Aldo had named the shore house Diamond Dunes. It was clear why she and Frank had never ever worried about their finances. It was clear why Frank was so insistent that she change nothing until he returned.

She put everything back in its bag or box, then carefully she put it all back into the laundry basket and took it back downstairs to the safe. There it would stay until she decided what she wanted to do with it all.

The tiara, that was easy. She'd keep that for Robin. Sapphires to march the color of Robin's eyes. One day, Robin would need it. Not now, granted, but Robin's time would come sooner than anyone wanted it to come. It would be a bittersweet moment, and Suzanne hoped sweeter than not for everyone involved. The coins -- she would sell those to a dealer as she needed capital. The gems, oh God, that sounded difficult and risky, but she would deal with that as well someday, but not tonight. The Florentine Diamond – the diamond that should not have disappeared a century before? She'd keep it and hold it occasionally for the thrill of it, for sharing this one last thing with Frank. But in her heart, she already knew it had to go back to Austria, back to Vienna. Someday, but not too soon.

Once it was all locked away again, and the lights were out, Suzanne went up the basement steps, the bottle of wedding champagne in her hand. In the kitchen, she set it on the counter, took a towel and wiped off twenty years of dust and put it into the refrigerator. Later she'd drink it, just her and all the happy memories of Frank she could conjure up.

For she was free. Free of the fetters of having promised 'Forever' to Frank when he had not meant she should keep that promise beyond his passing. Free from having promised to never change anything. She would stay in this house, but now was free to make it her own, to move forward.

Tomorrow she'd start anew. But tonight, she was exhausted from the events of the week, and emotionally drained by the knowledge of all that had gone on without her knowing, back before she was married to Frank and up until his death. Plain and simple exhaustion.

Right now, it was time for a shower, some comfortable lounging clothes, and then that chilled bottle of bubbly to celebrate her memories of her time with Frank and her new Forever.

The Diamond Dunes Murders

Shelly Young Bell worked in industry as an Art Director and Director of Communications while also pursuing her writing. Most recently, she is the author of *The Phoenix Mysteries,* a series of novellas and short stories set near her home in Doylestown, PA. and *Stand Like the Brave,* a Historic Fiction book about a shell-shocked WW1 vet facing WW2.

Facebook: Shelly Young Bell, Mystery Writer
https://www.facebook.com/pg/ShellyYoungBell/

Books by Shelly Young Bell

The Phoenix Detective Mysteries
A Very Sisterly Murder, Book 1
Murder at St. Katherine's, Book 2
The Diamond Dunes Murders, Book 3
The Cabot College Murders, Book 4
Population 10, The Dead End Murders, Book 5
R.S.V.P. to Murder, Book 6
Murder on the Promenade Deck, Book 7
Murder at 13 Curves, Book 8

Historic Novel
Stand Like the Brave

All available on Amazon under Shelly Young Bell

Made in the USA
Middletown, DE
13 November 2023